SCHROEDER

BOOKS BY NEAL CASSIDY

the final weekend: a stoned tale

SCHROEDER

First published in 2024 by M & S publishing.

This is a work of fiction. All of the characters, incidents, and
dialogue, except for incidental references to public figures, products,
or services, are imaginary and are not intended to refer to any
living persons or to disparage any company's products or services.

ISBN: 979-8-218-47116-3 (paperback)
ISBN: 979-8-218-47117-0 (ebook)

Typeset in Berling

Cover Design and typesetting by Jamie Keenan.

nnaight@yahoo.com

SCHROEDER

neal cassidy

for my mom, carey, & scrapdog...

"i am who i am not,
but who i wanted to be..."

Neal Cassidy

SCHROEDER

so as to require ingenuity in ascertaining its answer or meaning to make your way comfortably ...ays somehow wrong...any attempt to make your way to people who weren't ...way to convey a powerful memory to people who weren't ...with the

altschmerz – : noun a sense of weariness, especially ...become worse or more intense, especially ...getting noun : the feeling that time is getting **zenosyne** – noun : an illuminating discovery, realization or disclosure the fortunes of a person or organization after a long period **fester** – verb : ...associated with rainfall, especially after a long period of warm, dry weather ...noun : the feeling that ...the lowest point in the fortunes of a person or organization **aulsy** – noun : a que... **nadir** – noun : th... been gnawing on for decades you've been gnawing on for decades

riddle **paro** – noun : a memory will become a memory this moment ...ring some invisible taboo ...will become a memory ...issues and anxieties you've ...the same boring issues and anxieties you've always had, the same old problems that you've always had, the same ...through the world will only end up crossing some invisible taboo there at the time **des vu** – noun : the awareness that this moment will become a memory ...the world will only ...faster as you get older through long-term neglect **koinophobia** – noun : the fear that you've lived an ordinary life ...neglect or indifference **petrichor** – noun : a pleasant smell that frequently ...which it is difficult to find one's way **epiphany** – noun : ...a complicated irregular network of passages or paths in which **labyrinth** – noun : a complicated irregular network of passages or paths in w...

LIKE EVERY MORNING, THE NEIGHBOR'S dog's constant barking wakes me up prior to my alarm, and without needing to look out the window I can picture Magnum standing on his wooden deck, halfway through the sliding glass door, refusing to move despite his owner's pleas. Purchased under one condition made by the mother of the children—that it be named after a character played by her Hollywood crush, Tom Selleck—the little white mutt would growl incessantly at nothing for minutes until Sam, the family's golden retriever, squeezed past him onto the deck, invariably prompting Magnum to leave the doorway hurriedly, chasing Sam to bite him from behind, snarling and persistently pulling his tail on the way to the stairs leading to the backyard.

Still completely covered by my sheets and shifting out of my sleeping tiger to a supine position, I chuckle nonchalantly in the darkness while recalling the previous Saturday evening when I was ruminating on my life in one

1

of the faded green plastic chairs on my patio, my epiphany unknowingly just around the corner, seconds away, the panacea that might prove to be the tweak to possibly solve all of my problems, proving that I was more than a product of my circumstances—*In his backyard, Magnum was barking at Tundra, a Samoyed quadruple his size, a daily ritual, but this time Tundra jumped her fence and attacked him. Hearing his buddy's cries, Sam, who was sunning himself on the deck, slowly rose from his slumber, leisurely ambled to the bottom of the stairs, and then, like lightening, bolted off towards Tundra, unleashing a violent fury on the dog who was mauling his tiny, best friend. Tundra's coat, usually a brilliant white, became tinged with blood as she helplessly yelped and tumbled to the grass before limping back towards her yard, ending the fight, which never really was one, and, on their way to the deck Magnum briskly ran to catch up with Sam solely to bite his tail, snarling and waggling it like he always did.*

Groggy after not sleeping well for the fifth night in a row, my muscles and joints sore, aching as if I'm ill with a cold even though I'm not, I yank the sheets off my head, snatch my phone from the edge of the Cargo nightstand I was gifted one random childhood Christmas, deleting the alarm that I seldom require, and stretch my arms and legs, savoring the final bit of comfort and security of my warm bed. Disregarding my desire to stay a tad longer, I reach to the same table, slip on my glasses, and glance from the photo of me and my mom taken eight years ago at my high school graduation to the stain on the ceiling that appeared last week and seems to have worsened, then to the poster below it with the garage full of Porsches and immense beach mansion, "JUSTIFICATION FOR HIGHER

EDUCATION" written in bold, neon lettering at the top. I reverse the spelling in my mind, **NOITACUDE REHGIH ROF NOITACIFITSUJ**, jolt my head back, cracking my neck, and peek through the partially closed blinds above my desk to check the weather. The past two days had been unseasonably cool and inclement, supposed to be more of the same today, at least that's what the forecast predicted, and it's cloudy, drab, but not as somber as yesterday, giving me faith this day will be better, that I won't be forced to contend with rain.

Last night I had that reoccurring dream where I'm naked in public wandering the streets among a crowd of strangers with some imaginary errand to run or task to accomplish, and I can't explain why this nightmare repeats itself in different communal scenarios or why I'm naked, but I'm relieved I didn't have the one that has me in an awful panic, perpetually sprinting down a never-ending school hall clutching an overdue, fictitious homework assignment that will stop me from graduating. I swing my feet to the floor, slide on my socks and striped headband, grab the yellow JBL speaker from my desk drawer, pair it with my phone, turn the volume up too loud, and place both beside the circus hot air balloon lamp atop the wooden, black entertainment center before flipping the TV and PS4 on and scrolling through my list of movies until I find, *Heat.* Fast-forwarding to the climactic, shootout scene and muting it so it doesn't interfere with my music, the chaotic centerpiece of the film begins with silent, heavy-caliber gunfire flashing on the screen and filling the streets as I tug at my grey V-neck then grasp my small belly, jiggling it slightly, and not regretting having eaten an entire medium pepperoni-and-sausage pizza with two canned Cokes for dinner yesterday, I align my feet together, inhale deeply, press "play" on my phone, and quickly stick my hands to my hips before Elton John's "I'm Still Standing" begins blasting from the speaker, the music motivating me to rock slightly and shake my right leg out of habit. I'm a terrible dancer, so I continue just swaying rhythmically, and the instant he utters his first words I perform a short hop, spread my legs, and raise my arms to ninety degrees, ready for my workout. GNIDNATS LLITS MI. Abruptly, and in a choppy motion that's probably not good for my lower back, I touch each foot with my opposing fingers, doing a hundred reps, fifty per side, then march from wall to wall, raising my knees to my chest, not rushing it like my previous exercise, which I don't particularly enjoy. Lighting up the screen, bullets fly, decimating everything in their path, littering cars with holes, shattering windshields, and the song ends during my eleventh trip, but restarts because I put it on repeat, so I maintain this exercise, eventually concluding my six-minute and four-second workout once it's finished again, since that's how long it takes for the song to play twice. Not raising the sound on the TV (carnage still ensuing—a policeman is shot dead in a parking lot as a couple of the bank robbers narrowly escape in a station wagon), I pivot on my heel, swiveling to spot my reflection from the side in the mirror, the unappealing sight of my sagging tighty-whities and protruding belly inducing me to suck it in, puff up my chest and flex my skinny arms while imagining the shape I'd be in if I made the effort to exercise more or incorporated weights. Well aware I won't have the time now, I relax my body, my stomach hanging over the tight

4

band on my underwear, and, not particularly dissatisfied with what I see, I shrug in resignation and make my bed, pulling at the corners of the red plaid comforter until the wrinkles disappear, situating my pillows the same way I regularly do, then set Sweet Lou on the ones on the left facing the window, the section I sleep on, balancing him so that he doesn't topple during the day.

Following our visit to the Capital, our fifth-grade teacher gave us twenty minutes in the gift shop to pick out what we wanted to buy as souvenirs. While all the other boys rummaged the store seeking fake guns, rifles, military hats, uniforms, and bows and arrows, I was searching for something unique to buy with the twenty dollars my mom had surprised me with this morning when she handed me the paper-bag lunch she'd packed. But I wasn't sure what. I scanned the items in the aisles, looking and not touching, unintrigued by the pens, coins, clothes and miscellaneous merchandise bearing images of Washington D.C. landmarks such as the White House, the Capital, and various other buildings I couldn't identify, and pretty soon I found myself perusing a card stand, contemplating that it might be nice to get my mom a postcard that she'd be able to pin on the refrigerator next to the picture I'd drawn of the Sun and a rainbow with a bunch of clouds and birds a month ago, a keepsake she'd cherish like the drawing. But I knew what she'd say if I did, that it was so kind, but she wished I'd bought a toy or picture book for myself, so I don't, then I suddenly heard, "Children, you have five minutes!" and feeling panicky about the premise of disappointing her by not bringing home a souvenir she knew I'd benefit from, I promptly spun around, accidentally knocking into the stand. Knowing it would waste precious time, I scooped up the mess I'd created from the floor, *placing the cards and envelopes back on the stand, hoping I arranged them correctly and they matched, and after hastily stuffing several red envelopes behind postcards with the Lincoln Memorial on them, I notice a stuffed animal display hidden by a tree adorned with D.C. ornaments and red, white, and blue ribbons. I'd never really been interested in stuffed animals, but I inadvertently wandered that way regardless, a heightened sense of urgency growing in me, my riddle of what to get still unsolved, and not particularly impressed by the fluffy stuffed eagles and donkeys and elephants in front of me, I scoured the pile, tossing bodies aside, and that's when I saw him jammed between a lion and an elephant, his head scarcely visible—a stuffed wooly mammoth. Maybe ten inches long and eight inches tall, with dark, caramel fur, a peanut-brown face, trunk, ears, feet, and ivory tusks, he was the cutest and neatest thing I'd ever seen in my nine-year old life, and I immediately knew I had to have him. Keeping my fingers crossed, I urgently plucked him from the pile, anxious to check if his price exceeded twenty dollars, and I smiled the hugest smile I'd had in forever when I saw $9.99, then, for a scant moment, I remembered how I could now buy a lunch with the rest of the class at McDonald's instead of eating the ham and cheese sandwich and chips and apple my mom had packed for me, but that brought me nowhere near the happiness the wooly mammoth did, so, focusing on him, I excitedly whipped my money out of my pocket before skipping to the register, and while I was bouncing up and down, my clenched fists near my chest in anticipation as I waited for the sweet lady with the name badge that read "NeNe" to cut off the tags after I'd asked her to, I heard our teacher yell from the entrance, "Ok, students! On the bus!"*

When we arrived at the Washington Monument I propped my wooly mammoth on a stone marker, casually hopping, then hurdling him beyond invisible obstacles, imitating whooshing, flying noises as I did. "What a dork," David shouted, laughing, in an attempt to call me out in front of my classmates, then nudging his buddy, Bill, he aimed his guns at me and shot me four times, twice with each gun in alternating order, a "pew-pew" continually flowing from his lips, which was ridiculous because it made him sound more like a laser gun rather than a real gun. The boys with him started to laugh, none of them raising their guns or bows and arrows, only pointing and mocking me, but it didn't upset me the way it normally did, so, simply disregarding them, I vaulted my furry new companion into the air while inventing different, new noises, I haven't the faintest idea what, just not some stupid, laser sound, and that same smile I had in the gift shop returned.

Once the driver reversed the bus into the parking lot and all the other students eagerly ran off to form a jumbled line so they could choose what to order at McDonald's, I stayed in my seat and happily opened the brown paper-bag with my name written on it in capital letters, print, that my mom had packed for me. I pretended to feed my ham and cheese sandwich and a chip to my new friend, then, prior to falling asleep while hugging him tightly on the bus against my teacher, Miss Joni, since nobody ever wanted to sit with me, I decided to name him Sweet Lou after a character I'd briefly seen in a skateboarding-themed movie that my mom had caught me watching and made me change as soon as she'd realized it was PG-13.

The purple-and-green tiled shower feels smaller than it truly is when I step in, close the glass door, like yesterday, and the day before, but today I ignore it, not dwelling on its constrictiveness, letting the warm, cozy water hit my torso, head, and back while I calmly spin twice, embracing the toasty, well-pressured stream as it comforts me, finding it slightly amusing that I didn't want to get in here at first and now I don't care to leave. Despite the shower not growing, my usual seven-minute bath extends to fifteen, the majority of it spent with my eyes shut standing in place until I finally wash my hair then my face with the Darth Vader-shaped charcoal soap, doing both in a hurry. After drying off haphazardly, I fold the purple towel neatly, straightening it on the rack alongside the matching washcloth I only use for my hands, spray the shower tiles with the tile cleaner that doesn't require scrubbing, and apply two dabs of pomade to my thick, chestnut curls, before running my fuchsia brush that's missing half a handle from the time I snapped it in high school preceding what I'd deemed a bad hair day in ninth grade through it, parting it to the left while considering the word "fuchsia," and how I fancy it, the way it sounds when I pronounce it; however, I rarely have a use for the word seeing as the color isn't popular and most people aren't familiar with it, anyway, then the words "cellar door," enter my thoughts and I recall an article I once read in USA Today that quoted a renowned linguist who said it was the most sublime example of euphonic sound combination in terms of phono aesthetics, but I never understood it, the beauty, and returning to my bedroom, I open my closet. Plopping into the chair that I play video games and watch TV in, I slide on my khaki pants with no pleats and the pink, collared Criquet shirt I'd specifically bought to wear today after seeing one of my favorite actors, Luke Wilson, modeling one in an online ad, and I'd dwindled my account to $23.46 for it, then I slip into my socks and my grey New Balance shoes, creating bunny loops to tie them because I didn't bother to learn the other way as a child, double-knotting them so they won't unlace.

Slowly revolving the leather seat with my feet inch by inch, my interlocked fingers cupped in my lap, I swivel around in circles I'm not certain how many times before eventually stopping and gazing blankly at my black backpack and the beige, cylindrical tube I'd packed last night. Sitting in the corner, I'd purposefully avoided acknowledging them with the intention of not disrupting my morning routine, but I've now reached that juncture, if I'm going to do this I must go, then, unexpectedly, the realization of how I've led an inferior existence, not really done anything of significance in my life is brought to my attention again this week—how my lived experience would look so inconsequential if I were to put it on paper—and, not helping at all, life has been creating the impression that it's zooming by faster and faster, especially after last week. I sink deeper into the chair at the recognition and acceptance of this, my shoulders feeling heavier, my entire body tired, chronically fatigued from the last nine days, and catching my eye, the stain is larger, dirtier and seems to be creeping across the vinyl tiles in my direction, unnerving me even more, so I glance fleetingly at the poster of the Porsches in an effort to divert my unconstructive, negative mindset, **NOITACUDE REHGIH ROF NOITACIFITSUJ**, wait a few seconds, but my pessimistic contemplation hasn't dissipated and neither has the stain, in fact it's expanded and nearing me, and now sensing the recognizable beginning of a possible migraine, I rush to the bathroom, splash some water on my face. Staring into the mirror, examining the faintest of lines under my eyes, the gray strands in my hair, it vaguely troubles me how they weren't there and suddenly were, much like the stain on my ceiling, and out of nowhere, the festering weariness of the same, old issues I've had, endlessly, my whole life, the persistent, boring flaws and anxieties that have been gnawing at me for years—my appearance, my lack of self-confidence, the belief that no matter what I do it's somehow constantly wrong, that any attempt to make my way comfortably in this world will only be met by various, invisible taboos—pop into my head, provoking the throbbing to worsen. I grip the sink with both hands, drops of water trickling from my chin and splattering the green porcelain, my melancholic trance worsening, my angst rising like boiling water, my dread unfocused on the state of the world as my awareness that I'm at the lowest phase of my existence envelops me, so I unlatch my cabinet mirror in the middle and pop three of my pills in my mouth, swallowing them whole with no water, collapse in my gaming chair, close my eyes, start humming to myself while rocking, and after a bit of time trying not to think about anything, anything at all, I feel better.

The urgency of the day dawns on me as I open my eyes and wonder how more than ten minutes have elapsed, so, choosing to forget how I felt earlier, I jump out of my seat, return to the bathroom with a determined gait to brush my hardened curls, styling them neatly so they don't stick out, and, as pleased as I can be with how I regularly look, I groom my mustache, probing for wild or uneven hairs, but there are none because I'd trimmed it with my electric shaver when I cut my nails yesterday in the shower since they're easy to wash away once I'm done. Turning to the side, I briefly observe my nose in the mirror like I do every morning, specifically where it protrudes in the middle, revalidating the reality of how obtrusive it is when I view it from this angle, why people sporadically ask me if I've broken it, then, like always, I face forward, reassuring myself unconvincingly that I'm not as ugly from this perspective, and, ignoring the folded five-dollar bill on my dresser that I allow myself for daily expenses since I won't have a need for it today, I grab my yellow Member's Only jacket from the coat rack, gather my bag, the tube, and, still kind of groggy and lethargic, not altogether there yet, meander to the top of the stairs, bumping against the wall on my way to the door above me as if I'd just learned how to walk.

Like a lot of things I do, I utilize a system for cooking breakfast, one that maximizes my time, ensuring my food is ready and will remain hot by simultaneously washing the utensils I cooked it with while I heat my meal for an additional forty-seven seconds in the microwave, and once I've scrubbed and cleaned the skillet and spatula, finishing as the buzzer dings, I'm prepared to eat with no interruptions because I'd packed everything that was essential for today last night, so I send Harry his email, ignoring the news notifications pertaining to the fire that killed thirty in Portland, Monday's mass shooting at a train station that was stopped by a policeman and a college professor, the bombing in Europe, and rotate the white plate with a pair of navy stripes bordering its edge that I use for most meals to separate my scrambled eggs far enough from my whole wheat toast with peanut butter and honey so they don't touch, then pour a glass of orange juice. Sliding issue #3 of *The Amazing Spider-Man*, **NAMREDIPS GNIZAMA EHT**, out of its plastic sleeve, I admire the cover, passingly remembering when I purchased it with the money I had after selling my computer in the sixth grade from the blonde, shaggy-haired, pudgy owner of the comic book store that was basically his home, the first and only single-digit number of my Spider-Man comic book collection, and blindly nibbling on one of the halves of toast and sipping on my juice using my right hand, I flip the pages with my left to be extra careful, my eyes glued to the comic as I lean on the table awkwardly and unnecessarily while periodically adjusting my glasses to read, not out of necessity—it gives me the impression that I'm more absorbed, that I'm scrutinizing and relishing every illustration, line, and word in each frame as they're meant to be, so I won't need to read it again, like a song I wasn't appreciating and have to restart. Normally when I eat I grip the Achilles tendon on my left leg with the big and second toe from my right foot, squeezing and massaging it, a habit that makes me feel comfortable, secure, but I can't on account of my shoes which I didn't want to deal with post-breakfast and that I'm not supposed to be wearing in the house, and done on purpose I finish my last bite of food as I read the final page, then after I've washed and dried the dishes and made sure my fingers are totally clean and not moist, I slip the comic back in its sleeve, throw on my jacket then my backpack while doublechecking the cuckoo clock to ensure I'm on schedule—and I am; it's 7:59—so I wait, my head sinking and eyes focusing on the tiled, kitchen floor for the seventeen ticks of the curvy, blue hand it entails, and not sounding anywhere close to how she usually does, grainy, I hear, "Goodbye, Sweetie. I love you," from the living room, and I slide the door shut behind me.

The bleak, dreary clouds and gloomy conditions destroy my hope of feeling the morning Sun on my skin following a night inside, but the air is ripe with the gratifying, dewy petrichor of the rain, eclipsing this negative thought, and, despite it being overcast, there are no signs of a storm, so I don't worry about the umbrella I used yesterday that's leaning against the potato-and-onion bin in the pantry I now realize I forgot, and trudge sluggishly to the bottom of the patio stairs, my footsteps heavy and sedated, zombielike, towards the garage. Packed yesterday after my exercises, the box our floor heater came in is on the workbench I paint my action figures on, but prior to adding the final item, the cherry on top, I recheck the contents, confirming nothing's misplaced and everything's where it should be, guaranteeing it will be received exactly as I want, and wrapping it in last year's Christmas paper covered in dogs wearing Santa suits and hats that I'd found in the closet and put out with the tape and scissors last night, I add a pink bow as a joke when I'm done, sticking it in the center. I tie a Velcro strap around my pant leg, ensuring it won't get caught in the chain, revealing my dark socks with multiple, red skulls and crossbones on them, then set the present in the handy wicker basket at the front of my cruiser bike, lock the garage door, and cautiously loop the tube's strap on my shoulder, freezing up as I do. Realizing I forgot to oil my chain this week with all that was going on, I don't concern myself with the squeaking as I steer between my home and the neighbor's fenced yard while the kind, elderly widow that moved in a decade ago begins waving at me from her patio, the sleeve of her customary flowered gown wriggling down her arm, and shyly nodding I unintentionally recollect the man with the angry, intimidating dog who'd lived there before her when I was a kid—the stout, mean soul with jet-black hair and a moustache that absorbed light, who kept my balls and frisbees that landed in his fenced-in backyard and shot his wife—not in this house, their next one—then, changing direction, I swerve under the oak tree with the rope swing that we planted when I was eleven, riding down and up the ditch onto the pavement, to the end of Cornelia, which comes quick since there's only two homes between mine and the corner, so, extending my left arm, I bend it at a ninety-degree angle while decelerating to a full stop.

Biking by the familiar vinyl-sided ranch homes and split foyers on Poplar Drive, the ranch with the German Shepherd that used to dart out of its garage to trot along the edge of its lawn barking and chasing me when I was growing up floats by, its occupants long gone, a young family recently settled in, and while coasting down the steep, lengthy hill, past the unfinished Craftsman house that's been under construction for years, I visualize myself from the sky, my cruiser navigating its way through the labyrinth of streets like I'm in a video game as it squeaks with every rotation of its pedals, avoiding barking dogs, noisy, obnoxious motorcycles, drivers distracted on their phones, when an ominous melody for the day gradually starts materializing and building in my head, the music getting louder and louder. Some sinister symphony I recall having heard previously, I'm not certain when or where, maybe a movie soundtrack, and now, nearing the bottom of the hill, the wind hitting my face, hopefully not disheveling my gelled curls, for no reason in particular I begin reflecting on that song, "Once in a Lifetime" by Talking Heads, how I'd adored it in fifth grade and dressed up as the singer from the video for a Halloween competition despite no classmate in school knowing who he was, only the teachers, and I can envision my mom fixing my bowtie that morning, the one she'd happily bought to appease my insistence that it be real, and her crying and me asking why and her telling me it was nothing, just that she wished I could stay this way forever, and it truly saddens me that I have nobody to convey this type of sorrow to, but even if I did, they'd be incapable of comprehending its meaningfulness because they weren't there at the time. Arriving at the intersection of Poplar and Jefferson I stand there with my bike between my legs facing the entrance to the pool we could never afford, where laughing families unload their cars and SUVs packed with coolers, folding chairs and towels, as two shirtless boys hiding amongst a clump of bushes shoot water pistols at each other, their excited sister bouncing in place nearby, a tiger-printed float already around her waist, eager for the pool, and I know my first appointment is left, so I should signal whether or not there's a vehicle or people nearby, but I don't because I don't want to, I simply go, when not too far down the road, while struggling to convince myself that I possess the strength and courage to walk into that bodega, the depressing truth I reflected on earlier reenters my consciousness—how inconsequential my life has been, what little I've accomplished, how my days have appeared to slip by faster and faster as time has progressed, and suddenly the jolting awareness that *I am going to die*, that these passing years haven't been a dress rehearsal, hits me, and I try to shake it but I can't, and after another two miles I reach T. Hardy's Market without thinking about anything else.

Even though I'm on the farthest, right edge of the curb, an Asian woman in a visor honks at me unnecessarily while racing by in a maroon delivery van at a much speedier pace than the 25-mph limit, and when I coast into the paved lot, an older-model blue Range Rover is the sole car there. I lay my cruiser against the upscale bodega's brick wall, not fussing with chaining it to the bike rack since I won't be but a minute, then while verifying the time—8:19—on my watch, I catch a brief glimpse of the tags on the Range Rover. "**CHEFFIN**." "**NIFFEHC**." Rounding the corner, an aging couple walking a Chihuahua stop, and smile, wave, I reciprocate, and the dog startlingly begins jumping and yipping, yanking at the leash while eyeing a hissing white cat in a tree. Holding the miniature dog at bay as they take the crosswalk, the husband slides his arm around his wife's waist, swapping spots with her so she's away from traffic, and pulling out my yellow, subject notebook #32—I'd been gifted a yellow notebook by my mom on my tenth birthday to use as a diary, an exercise she told me would help inspire creativity, improve my writing, allow me to keep my ideas, deliberations and sentiments organized—I flip through the filled pages to a blank sheet, when my cell phone rings, so I peek at it hastily, but it's merely a robocaller, I receive numerous such calls daily, and annoyed my train of thought's been distracted I shove it back in my pocket, press the paper down so none of it is entangled in the metal spiral, write the date, 8:19, the number 2, and stuff it in my bag. Grabbing the tube, I carefully position the cylinder so it's in front of me while apprehensively scanning the area to reconfirm there's nobody around, that the pair and their dog can no longer be seen, and with a deep breath, I adjust my glasses, ignoring the sign that lists the bodega's daily operating hours, 9AM to 9PM, and push on the door.

The silver bell overhead dings as I fling it open, and the bulky Black man with the fluffy, grizzled beard on the opposite side of the counter notices me straight away, but he carries on yelling at the other guy in the market, who's also Black and works there. "And if a girl rejects you, you don't try again later, Mike!" he exclaims, laughing, chuckling at himself while banging the counter three times, causing the boxes of mints on the register to totter and the water in the fish tank at the end of the counter to vibrate as bubbles shoot out of the pirate's chest near a diver in a copper helmet that's swaying back and forth on the multicolored pebbles, striped clownfish circling him, then the man's expression switches from joy to contempt when he turns to me, slamming his palms on the counter and narrowing his eyes. "Nice helmet, douchebag. What the fuck are you doing here? Neither of us lik—," and I can't understand what else he says. It sounds muffled for some reason, distorted, maybe I'm preoccupied with everything that's recurring in my mind— what I'm compelled to do today, each place I must get to, the limited hours I have to execute it all if I can—but it's emphatic and abrasive and familiar, then pointing his finger at me, he shouts additional insults, his chuckling friend joining him in mocking me and laughing while barely mopping the wooden floor, and I'm not sure why, but I'm more nervous than I expected to be, fidgeting with the lid of the cylindrical container that should be effortless to remove, popping it off at last. Wriggling the strap from my shoulder and clutching what's inside, I release the tube, revealing what's in my possession, impelling the gigantic man's eyes to widen instantaneously, and the next few anxious moments seem to tick by in slow motion as I raise the shotgun, aiming it at him, his formerly confident, unkind facial expression contorting drastically into one of confusion and fear, his hollering immediately changing to a stuttered stammering I still can't register. Tentatively raising his shaking arms, he takes two wobbly paces backwards. "Wha—, what the fuck are you doi—" When I squeeze the trigger, the gun doesn't kick with as much force as I'd presumed, and the man flies back into the display case of candies and gums on the wall behind him, collapsing the drawers and shattering the mirror, his hefty frame crashing to the floor with a hard thud. A bright hail of numerous yellow, green, red, blue, and orange M&Ms and Skittles shower him from above, randomly spilling onto his white, collared shirt that's now painted in arterial red, and scattering on the floorboards all around him, producing a chaotic mass of repetitive pings as his dead, panic-stricken eyes stare towards me, past me, at nothing. With his arms caught on fractured shelves and dangling at shoulder height, both wrists limp, his head slumps to the side, evoking images of a hay-stuffed, crucified scarecrow in the middle of a corn field in my mind, while his mangled nose swings by a tiny, veiny thread and chunks of his chin cling to what remains of his jaw, which is now mostly pink and purple strands of muscle hanging from splintered bone, then a stream of magenta and brown liquid mixed with what I can only guess is probably saliva or mucus, some lemony film, starts flowing from what used to be his mouth, saturating what's left of his split, holey beard, and I can't help but be conscious of the fact that this—the here and now—will ultimately become a memory, like everything else I've done in my life, and–

"Jesus Christ! Chris! Jesus Christ! What the fuck?!" Mike squeals, reminding me of what else I came to do, so, pointing the shotgun in the direction I'm looking, I spin swiftly to my left, the barrel passing over the freshly baked bagels and bread, until it's aimed at my second target, who's shrieking, "No, no!" With wide eyes and his mouth agape, he drops the mop and the clear plastic cup of soda he's holding, the phone in his other hand following them, the rap music emanating from its speakers not stopping when it bounces off the wood, and he gawks frantically from me to Chris, back to me. "Please, please don't." Petrified, with tears trickling down his dark-skinned face and his entire body convulsing, his legs, his arms, his knees, he timidly raises his trembling hands, but he doesn't attempt to escape. He can't. He's frozen. Without hesitating, I step forward for maximum effect, hoisting the gun and pulling the trigger without a hint of trouble, not a care, preventing him from uttering one more word, because I don't want to hear it, or even acknowledge it, and his camouflaged, army-style hat is sent straight into the air when his head all at once transforms to a rosy, mushy mess as blood and pieces of his skull and brain splatter a frosty refrigerator door and the rack of magazines behind him, spraying the muscled men and scantily clad women, cars, homes, and boats on the glossy covers. Resembling a Claymation figure the way he folds up at the knees and hips with such ease when his faceless body buckles, he sounds like some weighty sack hitting the floor, a bland thud that could be mistaken for a number of objects fallen, and there's a minute pause of silence on his phone before the next song begins, one as awful as the previous, with another rapper mumbling annoyingly, not legitimate rap, and, releasing the shotgun where I stand, I jerk my neck, cracking it, then, turning to enjoy the sight of the husky, fluid-leaking corpse lying at the foot of the counter, the comprehension of what I've done hits me, inducing a gradual smirk.

Knowing the fish won't be a priority once these two are found, and confident they weren't fed this morning, I uncap the orange bottle of food beside the fish tank and tap it mildly, spreading it across the water before strolling out the door, snickering when I hear the ding from the bell for the last time, and, gripping my handlebar, I wait while canvassing the area to determine whether a passerby or neighbor heard the gunshots, is possibly responding in any way, but everything's as normal and calm as it was two minutes ago and stays that way—traffic drives on by, three chatty kids roll through the intersection on skateboards, the same ravens that were perched on the telephone wires when I arrived remain, still squawking with each other—so, unworried, I lean down to secure my pant leg and realize there's no need, because like my helmet, with all that was

20

happening, I forgot to unravel it. Covering the circled number, I scribble an ornate red "X" on top of it, toss my notebook in my backpack, and when I reach the stop sign at the end of the road, my cruiser still squeaking, the sullen clouds appear to be vanishing, the Sun emerging from the fresher, white clusters moving in, and, experiencing a rush of optimistic anticipation mixed with a nagging, dreadful uncertainty of what's to come, I extend my right arm.

trumspringa – noun : the longing to wander off your career path in pursuit of simple

xeno – noun : the smallest measurable unit of human connection, typically exchanged between passing strangers

evanescence – noun : the quality of being fleeting or vanishing quickly

heartworm – noun : a relationship or friendship that you can't get out of your head, which you thought had faded long ago, but is still somehow alive and unfinished

rubatosis – noun : the unsettling awareness of one's own heartbeat

lagnappe – noun : something given as a bonus or extra gift

clinomania – noun : an excessive desire to stay in bed

lachesism – noun : the desire to be struck by disaster; longing for the clarity of disaster

kenopsia – noun : the eeriness of places left behind life

taradiddle – noun : pretentious nonsense

IT'S 2.54 MILES TO MY next objective, and I bike through this neighborhood's streets as if it's an ordinary morning, which it is for the pedestrians I'm pedaling by, the majority of whom seem bored or displeased, with sullen demeanors pasted on faces attached to semi-lethargic bodies just going through the motions, their heads facing downward and gazes focused on the concrete sidewalk, except for the middle-aged woman I pass (after the FedEx delivery man wheeling a dolly holding a sizable package out of the rear of his truck), who looks quite content on her knees in the garden of her modest yard, her blue rubber gloves caked in mud, but none pay me much notice, all of them carrying on about their business, nobody initiating a wave, let alone any type of simple greeting. It's funny how a smile from a stranger will brighten my day, instantly give me a jolt of excitement, a grin I didn't expect in an otherwise ordinary situation; however, none of these people seem to appreciate the same thing I do, not a single person registering me for longer than a scant glance, uninterested by my simple attempt at even the slightest of greetings.

I take a left, a right, another immediate left, and, leaning forward while occasionally balancing the cardboard box in front of me with one hand, I start biking harder, refusing to let this hassle me as I retrace my steps to what just took place, the images of their deaths unfolding in my thoughts on mute, no words, only actions, Chris's body hurling against the display case and mirror, Mike's head exploding like a piece of fruit, his moist, vermilion insides plastering his surroundings, and now feeling exhilarated and electrified, a surge of energy or light builds in my stomach, rises to my chest, goosebumps form on my arms. Picturing their horror-stricken expressions, then briefly conjecturing made-up, obscure choices that might have brought them where they were—standing at the counter and mopping while drinking a soda within the walls of that bodega at 8:19 AM—I wonder: even if they hadn't made the decisions that placed them there, if both of them had led completely different lives in separate states or countries with unrelated careers, one an insurance salesman in Pennsylvania, the other a teacher in Italy, would their deaths have transpired this morning, no matter what? A car wreck, a plane crash, some natural disaster, choking on a piece of meat…was it simply inevitable? Were they destined to die at 8:19 AM on June 29th, 2023?

After roughly half a mile I slow down considerably because I can't sustain the pace, but more importantly I don't want some sort of mishap to incur, spilling the contents of the box meant for my second stop, and, meandering my bike through the assorted, blotted shades of grey and black on the drying asphalt ahead of me so that I stay in the former and avoid the latter, I start to dwell on the movie I saw last night while I ate dinner in my gaming chair involving inmates that were held on various tiers of a vertical prison, two to a floor. It was in Spanish, so there were subtitles, but I didn't care, seeing as I opt for subtitles with every movie or show I watch so I don't miss a word, anyway, and there were upwards of three hundred stories and the prisoners were fed by a platform that lowered a gourmet buffet level by level every twenty-four hours, the purpose being to adequately feed all of them if each person took only his or her share for the day, but the food never travelled far, gluttony and a lack of compassion for others consuming the detainees in the loftier cells, inducing the inmates below to starve or kill themselves. The vinyl-sided and brick houses in this residential area eventually become offices and businesses in a downtown separated by Rainbow Forest School, my school from kindergarten through the eighth grade, now abandoned, a sight that was always odd for me to view in the summer, the forlorn atmosphere of buildings usually bustling with students and teachers currently empty, and I imagine myself in the tiered prison wearing the same tanned uniform the convicts had on, not in a despair-inducing position, but among the higher floors with the buffet lowering to my cell and me taking my turn, merely eating what I truly need for sustenance, a piece of chicken or beef and fruit, nothing more, before, prompted by the sight of the familiar property, I begin reminiscing about happy occurrences from my years there: a Halloween competition I won dressed as Alfalfa, eighth grade; the pillow that was supposed to be a baseball glove I sewed in home ec, sixth grade; field day at the end of school every June; lastly, impetuously and wistfully recalling my schemes from back then during days similar to yesterday, dreary mornings when I faked sick so I could laze at home, fulfilling my excessive hankering to stay warm and dry in my bed, finding peace indoors while I played video games and watched TV, mom well aware I was faking, but not caring, both of us oblivious these childhood incidents would be gone in the blink of an eye. I can't believe that Halloween competition was thirteen years ago—it's unreal to comprehend that each one—comprised of three hundred and sixty-five days, twenty-four hours apiece—at the moment felt long, now in retrospect, rolled by so inconceivably fast.

By the time I swing onto Church Street I'm once again reflecting on the little red-haired girl who immigrated here when I was in the seventh grade, an ephemeral friendship I've never gotten out of my head and that ended over a decade ago, yet still lingers, alive and unfinished. I have no idea why this continues to inadvertently reappear for me to ruminate on, a relationship that was so ancient, maybe because she was one of the few people in my life I remember genuinely being kind to me, and it doesn't surface often, probably every month or so, but it's remained with me since the day she left. A warehouse superintendent, her dad was concise with his words, large and intimidating to me at my age, and my mom encouraged me not to be nervous, look him in the eye when I visited, but I wasn't sure if it should be the left or right, so I'd shift back and forth between the two as he sat on the couch, iced vodka in hand, glued to the spot he seemed to never move from, while I waited for her to come jogging out of her room. Here for less than five months, we watched movies together, took walks around the neighborhood for hours habitually circling the same streets, ate ice cream on cones at the pond, she taught me how to say hello, goodbye, and politely ask for directions in Russian—the sole, true friend I had when I was a kid—and before she waved goodbye from the rear window of her family's minivan on October 6th, donning the unvarying clothes she dependably wore daily—jean shorts, Asics tennis shoes, that black t-shirt with an image of a chinchilla sporting aviator sunglasses, NILLIHCNIHC— we vowed we'd keep in touch regularly, pen pals forever, until we were old enough to reunite and recover our relationship, but she broke her promise, all of my letters to

Denver, unanswered, I question if ever read. Whenever she enters my mind, I wonder if she thinks of me on occasion. Do I drift into her thoughts without intention while she's reading a book, watching TV, driving her car? When a friend or significant other inquires about her past life, the various states and countries she was raised in, how she grew up, and she sooner or later mentions this place, a blip in the middle of her existence, does she reflect on what we had? If so, does she mention me? Like most people I've known, it's safe to say she doesn't, and if she did, she wouldn't.

Noticing I'm gripping my handlebars tighter with my now balmy palms I try to relax, steadily breathing in and out so I'm less likely to feel antsy in the shop, and Church Street isn't busy, which isn't much of a shock given that it's still early, the majority of the businesses' interiors dark with their doors locked, only the bakery and hardware store active, the bulk of the parking spaces that line the street empty, everything primarily quiet, except for the unnecessary, continuous construction that's become a staple of downtown, a sidewalk, road or median constantly being fixed, paved, or excavated, the bulk of them splurgy, exorbitant jobs invented to spend a projected, inflated budget in order to receive a monetary amount equivalent or higher to this year's for the next, and when I get to the temporary stop sign the light on top appears more intense than it really is, flashing irritatingly while the enormous bulldozer to my right repeatedly emits an abrasive, agitating beep, the driver reversing in my direction before slowly pulling forward to a sizable pile of sand near an obese man in a stained blue t-shirt with stringy, shoulder-length gray hair, who shakes his head as he pushes himself out of his chair to wave me by, his bright yellow vest hanging from the pole he's holding. On the ground close by, a beat-up radio speckled with white paint is playing a country song I can barely hear the lyrics to because of the noise, an opened energy drink and half-eaten candy bar lie beside it, and, to illustrate that he's undoubtedly annoyed, he makes a point of chuckling loud enough for me to hear, nodding and tipping his hat to me while I ride by, as if I've ruined his morning, absolutely inconvenienced him by interrupting his breakfast and forcing him to stand for five seconds, but I don't allow his negativity to unsettle me, instead I concoct an imaginary chain of events involving the bulldozer experiencing some type of malfunction at this very moment, causing it to lose its brakes or accelerate without warning, running me over, not enough to kill me or a serious scenario, just enough to put me in the hospital for a couple of days. I wonder who'd take the time to see me, drop by with the intention of visiting for the morning, afternoon, or an entire evening so I'm not alone. Would my room be full of flowers, balloons, and cards telling me to get well soon? But after signaling to designate a right turn, merging onto Main Street and gliding by the shoe store, Sweety Pie's, the courthouse, then decently hopping a speed bump, I ultimately decide it's silly and terrible to even consider an accident like that or an automobile crash or train wreck solely for attention, though it does seem nice knowing there are people concerned about your well-being, how you're doing, that they'd genuinely be upset if you were hurt, and while not bothering to admire the mannequins donning intense, shiny suits and vibrant hats with feathers sticking out of them in the show window of The Famous like I usually do, as a last ditch effort to justify my hideous urge to wish any actual harm on myself, even if temporary and purely for empathy, I picture a card propped on the table by my hospital bed next to a strawberry milkshake a fictitious buddy brought me. There's a silly caption or image on the front, nothing weighty or serious, and its eagerly unsealed, ripped envelope leans against a vase of roses so I can easily read the return address that's written in pink: 1014 Sherman Street, Denver, Colorado.

The comic book shop is around the corner, adjacent to the town's first cinema, which the Heritage Society is fighting to save from being purchased and converted into apartments by the Japanese real estate corporation that's building the new multiplex with thirteen screens, and I'm sweating, not profusely, but enough to warrant wiping my brow once I prop my kickstand as a guy hurriedly jogs from the other side of the road to his dented Toyota Corolla, slamming the door shut when he jumps in, then while backing up he bumps a Jeep Wrangler parked diagonally to him. Not troubling himself to get out and check if there's a hint of damage, he drives off apathetically, swerving as he fiddles on his phone, and I'm not sure why, but I'm suddenly feeling anxious, jittery, with no real reason to be, especially now that I've reached the point of no return. Standing between the multicolored brick walls in the dirty, narrow alleyway that leads to the shop's entrance, I'm reminded of my shower, how it's steadily been shrinking, and I'm positive that if I fixate on these rectangular blocks long enough this narrow passage will, as well, if I give it a minute or two, so ignoring that I don't want to, that I have no desire to see the outcome, I do and I wait, but surprisingly the alley stays the same, yet eerily quiet. I don't know why I do that, without fail invariably compel myself to select the choice I'm not partial to, like focusing on the stain earlier in my room, opting for a more difficult approach to perform a random task that should be uncomplicated, or coming to a decision in a manner I'd rather not to please others rather than myself. Maybe it's my faithful, foolish hope that by forcing myself to contend with matters in a challenging way I'm not fond of I'll get used to it, adjust, grow into a better person as a result, but in the end, I don't believe that's why, I think it's simply who I am, what I've always done. A gust of wind blows through, rustling and whirling stray papers into the air towards me, the soft swishing noise in the calm alley sounding so odd with the barely-there racket of the construction that was previously deafening, and, suddenly feeling for no reason or warrant as if I'm a thousand miles away in this paradoxical silence, I quickly ask myself several of the same questions I incessantly do, rapidly reeling off one after the other with no time to reply even if I could speculate an answer: Why was I denied any type of real, romantic relationship? Why do I have no children? No career I've risen in? How is it that nothing materialized for me at some stage in my life, an accomplishment or an attained goal that made me happy, completed me, or fell into place, explaining my purpose? Why am I broke with no real savings to speak of? Nothing that I can do anything of significance with like buy a house, take a trip, attend college. In addition to the recognition and admission of these recurring queries and affirmations that substantiate the fact that my existence has faded into inconsequentiality, a concern I've been mulling over this week in particular, one of my worst memories pops into my head and I ask nobody why I had to come back home that warm, spring night seven years ago from the sub shop to discover Scrapdog dead at the edge of our driveway, her gooey, shiny intestines spilling out of her split stomach, merely an object a stranger whose identity I'll never know crushed with their vehicle and kept on driving. Did they not see her? Were they truly oblivious? Or cognizant of a thud that caused the driver to glance hastily at the rearview mirror before continuing down the road without a care? What kind of person couldn't bother themselves to stop and at the minimum knock on my door or write a note? I threw my sandwich in the trash that night, abstaining from food while I cried for two days.

With this absolute jumble of obscure, noisy deliberations bombarding my brain, the alley remains quiet, the commotion of the orange bulldozer still a murmur, so I try to picture the colossal machine, its cab, the blade, the massive, rubber tires, but I can't, even though I was just there, similar to an object in the background of a photo that's fuzzy, it won't crystallize, then realizing that I'm breathing hard and my chest is pounding, the unsettling awareness of my own heartbeat abruptly enters my conscious, its throbbing echoing all around me, filling the tranquil air. Unable to help myself, I go with another decision I'm not partial to and raise my hand to my chest, craving to feel the thump, to match the beat to the sound. And I do, find the rhythm of my strong pulse, which, astonishingly, placates my current, restless mind, so I close my eyes, enjoy it a bit, the cadence of the vibrations I'm sensing with my palm urging me to nod my head to their rhythm. Unsure how many minutes have gone by, I'm eventually breathing normally again, so, swallowing a generous gulp of air and removing my hand from my heart with the understanding that I need to push through it, endure whatever else might bear down on me today and not distress myself over any of the daily life ruminations and realizations that perpetually hound me, I snap my neck, pull out my diary to scrawl the name of the comic book shop as well as the time below the preceding entry, and unaware of how many people this package will affect, in lieu of writing a number, I scribble a question mark with a smiley face.

The thought of what I'm about to do is something I would never have imagined doing last month, a year ago, but here I am lugging the heavy cardboard box against my chest, navigating my way between the maze of dirty puddles from this week's rain to the entrance, where a tall, lean man in his twenties in skinny jeans and a hoodie, who's talking on his phone, jumps a patch of water, then hurries in, letting the glass door covered in stickers click shut behind him, so, sighing, I turn around and open it with my butt, and the familiar smell strikes me when I step inside, but my pensive nostalgia isn't triggered in the same manner it normally is, and now suddenly more appreciative of the elation it used to give me, I'm briefly saddened by my unsatisfied desire to experience it like I once did. Despite the recent cool weather it's unusually toasty in here—the air conditioning broke five weeks ago and the owner is too cheap to pay what it costs to repair it. Instead he's ordered a part online that he's convinced will remedy the problem, and he's waiting for it to arrive so he can fix it himself. But it's extremely busy for the time of day regardless, for any time of the day, really, with over a dozen customers perusing the selection of the only comic book shop for sixty miles. The great thing about this store, what drives its success, is that it caters to both the serious collector, the lifeblood of the business, especially the ones with disposable incomes, and the casual fan, those who simply wish to buy new comics, models, or indulge on a sporadic whim. Ordinarily, it doesn't open until noon, most days it's later than that, but their annual sale is happening today—it began at 8 AM, ends at midnight. A well-known, traditional event that's guaranteed to attract lots of traffic, the entire inventory is now fifty percent off, twenty-five percent after 12:00, and will stay that way for the remainder of the day, except for certain comic books, obviously—you can't expect to acquire a coveted, vintage comic for half price—but the rest of the store—the models, action figures, posters, video games, everything else—is included in the sale, even the online, digital comics.

A high schooler in baggy clothing, his hat tilted to the side, slips his arm around the girl he's with as she thumbs swiftly through the middle of the "D" section then moves on to the "E"s. Seeming bored, she sighs and swats his hand away while two, eager teens rush by them, approaching the register. The guy in the hoodie strolls to the "DC comics" section, dark, go figure I guess, a woman wearing a beret and an aqua-and-black-striped shirt sips tea on the sofa near the fireplace I've never seen lit, and a hefty, Asian man with dyed blonde hair and green glasses meanders into the room to the left of the register with the humidifier and the lower lighting that holds the rare, expensive comics kept in sleeves with board backing, the issues serious collectors scour, making me curious what he's in search of—earlier, rare editions, or ones that introduce a future, prominent character, like the Punisher, **REHSINUP**, in *The Amazing Spider-Man #129*, or Wolverine in *The Incredible Hulk # 181*? **KLUH ELBIDERCNI EHT**. Walking between the rows of comics that are in alphabetical order in Bankers boxes, all of them in plastic, no cardboard, I'm satisfied with the number of clients here, prompting me to wonder who might be present when this is unwrapped, who will have made the decision to be a part of an unexpected consequence brought on by my actions. Delighted that at the very least it will involve the owner, I scan the rest of the dusty interior, secretly mostly hoping it will also impact someone like the Asian shopper as well, and as three of the fluorescent bulbs flicker above me, the same three that have been flickering for a month, a young boy, maybe nine or ten, yanks at his mother's arm, then grabs it with both hands, jerking and pleading for her to buy him something. "Come on, please. I promise if you get it for me I'll listen more." Hesitating, he struggles to formulate a strong argument that might entice her while tugging repeatedly. "I'll do my chores." Another pause. "Clean my room, do the dishes, walk Blackjack. Please, please, please, please."

Not giving him much of a fight, she manages, "Alex, you have dozens at home as it is," while already relenting to him, enabling his behavior by allowing him to drag her up the three stairs to the raised platform full of display cabinets lined with various, vinyl figurines and bobbleheads, where he excitedly snatches up a Funko Pop collectible of Scorpion, the undead ninja in Mortal Kombat.

Heading to the back of the store, past the racks of old, used video games and DVDs that are on sale for fifty cents, seventy-five at noon, to the roped-off "employees only" section, I push the tarnished gold turnstile when I hear vigorous clapping. "Hey! Hey! What the hell are you doing there in my office?" I twirl around quickly, the box still close to my chest, to find the slim, short, Indian owner, Remi, staring at me and wiggling his finger. "What are you bringing me, *fool*!?" he asks loudly in his usual, shrieking voice, emphasizing the word "fool," attracting the curiosity of every shopper. At the register ringing up the antsy youths, his silly antics cause the one with the mullet wearing a Hawaiian shirt, corduroy hat, and ripped jeans to tap his clueless friend in the bathing suit and Rob Zombie t-shirt, and with the three of them eyeing me I smile weakly, my hands clenching the cardboard tighter, unsure of what to say or how to respond, not eager to react in anyway, much less verbally, because that's the moment this conversation will become real and I want to avoid this. Realizing that I'm not going to counter, he scoffs and leans down from his elevated perch to mutter some tarradiddle to the boys, probably regarding me, while running his fingers through his thinning hair, his minimal pursuit of any type of human connection with me done for now, and relieved, I turn back towards his office, take a few, small shuffling steps even though I can do it in one, and nervously set the box on the metal desk Remi habitually occupies, his feet propped on it as he lounges in his chair sipping tea and bragging about the value of the limited-edition action figures on the shelf behind him, his collection of rare comics, or the fact that he has *The Amazing Spider-Man #1* (grade of 5.0) and *Batman #313* (grade of 6.5). Aligning the box with the edge of the desk, I straighten it so that it's an equal distance from each end, fluff up the bow, then pull the envelope meant for Remi out of the pocket of my Members Only jacket, his name written in lowercase letters, print, above a note: "do not read until 6!…unwrap after reading!", laying it on the box, and expecting him to follow the instructions and read it prior to receiving his special gift, my personal lagniappe to him for how he's unfailingly treated me, I happily envision the rest of his day, picturing him frantically helping customers and stocking comics with no time for his customary hour-and-a-half-long lunch break, completely oblivious to what the end of his shift will bring, and after taking in his self-proclaimed, open "office" one last time—the collection of figurines and autographed, encased football, basketball, and baseball cards on the shelves, the snapshots of him at various Comic Con's on his desk, the majority of them images of him with women in revealing cosplay costumes, the movie posters on the wall, John Carpenter's *The Thing*, the only one hanging in a frame, the ugly red and purple carpet, the Christmas tree decorated with colored lights in the corner that stays up and on all year, and, lastly, the puffy tan chair that whoever was across from him sat in—I set my index finger on the headrest, trailing it along and off the cheap leather before ambling through the turnstile, between the old video games and DVDs, down the row of comics, under the flickering bulbs, out the way I came to the door, flinching and grimacing when the owner yells in my direction as I grasp the handle. "That's right! Get lost, fool!" Chuckling at himself, he encourages the kids he's passing change to to laugh with him, which they hesitantly do, then, in a deep voice, he adds, "Enjoy your day," in a way that's meant to be funny, but oddly only sounds ominous, before pulling at the yellow collar under his burgundy Argyle sweater and winking while grinning mischievously just for me. I inspect the linoleum floor, adjust my glasses, and pursing my lips awkwardly, nod and wave goodbye, my subtle, persistent feeling of being amiss continuing to gradually grow with all these people around, and, inhaling slowly, I yearn for a single fond memory, emotion, or bit of nostalgia to emerge, produce a smile, but I don't expect it to given what's happened, and it doesn't, then, while I'm holding the door for a lady in her forties in a plaid business suit who appears disoriented, like she doesn't belong here, a disgruntled guy in line at the counter shifts his stance impatiently and tugs with frustration at his khaki cargo pants.

"Hey, is there another person working? I gotta be at an appointment. I've been standing in line for over two minutes," he complains, raising his hands to mimic quotation marks when he says, "two minutes," believing it adds significance to his statement, making me question if he truly has anywhere to be, or if the awful idea of needing to wait like any other customer is too much for him to bear.

Once I'm in the alley I cross out what I wrote in my diary prior to entering, haphazardly scribbling clumps of stars at the ends of the "X", combined with doodling that resembles fireworks while peering through the array of stickers on the glass door at Remi and his clientele going about their business as if I was never there, when the realization that I won't walk in there again is suddenly brought to my attention, the years I've spent inside reminiscent of the evanescence of ocean waves, here, then gone. I turn and stare at the brick walls as I did earlier, but this time I'm not fearing the alleyway shrinking or narrowing—for some mysterious reason, I'm imagining owning my own comic book store in another state or country with a major city. Not interesting me for long, my conjured-up images of skyscrapers and a city full of strangers soon dissipate, replaced by ones of a distant, idyllic land with lots of green hills and water, but also has a quaint town where I could operate my shop so customers could stop by while licking on ice cream in waffle cones or eating a popular, local pastry they'd purchased at the village market I'm unaware of because I've barely lived there a month. Visualizing the green, rolling hills and water, I dot them with fluffy white sheep instead of cows (despite cows having always been my favorite animal), flocks of them, clusters huddled together grazing on grass and weeds, the others off on their own doing whatever sheep do when they're not eating. What a simple, pastoral existence it would be, just tending to your herd, nothing more, nothing less, and I wonder if anyone had ever actually acted on an idea that began as a ridiculous farce, a self-proposal they were incapable of foreseeing themselves undertaking yesterday, and abandoned their career to become a sheepherder, relocated to a foreign country, leaving everything and everyone they knew, behind, and just as quickly as I conceived this scenario, my focus drifts to the sky that's progressively getting clearer, brighter, while I ponder what it might be like to pursue a lifelong dream in an effort to be the person you've always aspired to be, but the reality of the dreaded requirement of putting my true abilities out there to be judged by the open world, no longer protected within the secure bubble of my hopes and delusions, eventually creeps in, shattering any fantasy I'd have of attempting such an endeavor, knowing I couldn't endure the negative criticism, let alone waves of it. I would never possess the confidence in a million years, regardless of my talent, as if I'd ever even be endowed with an amazing skill, so I decide I'd be more of the sheepherder type, well aware I wouldn't do that either.

I hop from one leg to the next to my bike with extended lunges, jumping the puddles containing floating garbage discarded by people who lack the capability of finding a trashcan, then, crouching to fasten my pants, I see an elderly woman in a dark gown and flip flops watering the potted flowers and plants on her metal balcony two stories above me. Humming to herself jovially while dancing in place to her own rhythm as the tan curtains in her open entryway sway in the light breeze, she fluffs up her perfectly styled blueish hair, and noticing me harmlessly spying on her from below, waves nonchalantly, pausing her task for me to register her, so I stand and do. She returns to her garden, resumes her humming, and it seems odd to me that she's watering them given the recent, constant showers we've had, but it's none of my business what she does, maybe it's a routine she treasures, or perhaps they were indoors the last few days, either way I can't help but keep watching, taking in her blissful mood while she shuffles from flower to flower, plant to plant, her melody picking up in pace and volume as she trolls her personal sanctuary for vegetation she's missed, then, after I've watched for what is probably too long, she gestures merrily again, unbothered by my staring, this time not waiting for me to reciprocate before laying her watering can on a stool, spinning on her toes, and strolling inside.

My phone beeps, I can tell by the tone it's not a text message, and when I glance at the screen it's the latest news release: an Instagram model was found dead in her bedroom this morning in California; there's currently a mass tsunami in Japan; an update is expected later on the war in Ukraine, then, not caring in the way I previously did, I don't concern myself with avoiding the three puddles ahead, steering my cruiser through them rather than around them, the dirty water slightly splashing my pants legs, shoes, and socks. It's considerably easier to bike without the weight of the burdensome package in the wicker basket, so for my own entertainment I swerve and meander about the vacant street, waving to a young couple holding hands who nod back shyly, which is nice, the low noise of the construction dwindling until I can't hear it at all once I reach the toy store. Coasting leisurely across the rest of downtown, I exert the extra effort to absorb and appreciate the familiar surroundings I've known my entire life—the ice cream parlor where I'd habitually order a cone with two scoops, strawberry and mint chocolate chip, the barber shop Bob Carson cut my hair in, the humble sporting goods retailer that received the majority of its business from the local school teams, the dentist I'd gone to as a child with the kind, bearded man who kept a pirate chest full of cheap, plastic toys that I'd eagerly rummage after my appointment at the secretary's station—then, stopping at the last light on Main, three black puppies speckled with brown patches bounce playfully on woodchips in the window of the pet store, jumping on top of one another and tripping into their bowls of food and water, and about a hundred yards past that I cruise under the giant red banner that's connected to a bank and the post office and reads 10th Annual Garlic Festival in vivid gold with images of small American flags in all four corners, cartoon wine bottles and garlic cloves propped in and circling the letters. It doesn't take long to get to the other side of downtown, Main barely being half a mile in distance, and decelerating as I near its end to gaze through the window of Melvin's, the homely diner to my right where my mom and I ate breakfast every Sunday morning in the same booth, I crane my neck to keep our spot in sight as I ride by, eyeing the tabletop jukebox we dropped quarters in, then, with the diner leaving my view, before it's impossible to see anymore, I fling my head around and begin pedaling furiously up the steep hill towards one of the city's two wealthy neighborhoods.

diaphanous – adjective: (especially of fabric) light, delicate, and translucent

whipgraft deluion – noun : the phenomenon in which you catch your reflection in the mirror and get the sense that you're peering into the eyes of a stranger

views aquiver – adjective : quivering, trembling bellow – verb:(of a person or animal)

kerfuffle – noun : a commotion or fuss, especially one caused by conflicting

emit a deep loud roar, typically in pain or anger phosphene – noun: a ring or spot of light produced by pressure on the eyeball or direct stimulation of the visual system other than by light

sanguinolent – adjective : containing or tinged with blood toned – adjective : having firm and well-defined muscles

AHEAD ON MY LEFT, THE white-bricked entryway of Mols Country Club introduces a lengthy, paved drive flanked by evenly spaced purple and pink hydrangeas that winds through the golf course where I was employed as a caddy the summer I turned sixteen. My first job, I'd bike there before sunup at 6 AM to lug heavy bags for bad golfers all day, only to be thanked with encouraging words like "You work for me" and "This is my club," as well as a tip jar that was supposed to be shared, empty by the time I clocked out. Not much farther than that, on the opposite side of the road, I pass what was once the lone business in this part of town, Mitchell's, a family-run gas station renowned for its breakfast and fried chicken, now vacant after fifty years of serving as a staple of the community, yellow tape wrapped around its telephone poles and stretching across the parking lot to discourage drivers and pedestrians from entering. Bought by a local developer who's planning to convert it into luxury apartments, I'm prompted to reflect on the dramatic change this city has undergone in the last decade, growing in all directions—from more traffic lights, busier intersections, and the expressway built to save travelers time on their way north or south, to fields razed to make room for fresh neighborhoods and shopping centers holding a third CVS, a fourth McDonald's, or various other unnecessary buildings constructed so that people aren't forced to face the inconvenient problem of driving to the previously existing stores or restaurants that are two miles further away. Our community is littered with failed businesses that extinguished green areas—vacant properties with shattered signs and windows in overgrown parking lots—and after fleetingly, comically questioning why so many patches of undisturbed land have to disappear when there's plenty of available space that's been abandoned by shut-down establishments, despite my already knowing the answer—money—I'm feeling vaguely comforted by the sight of the familiar, aged cottage ahead that's been maintained for historic reasons, so I choose not to dwell on our city's current state any longer because it wouldn't do any good, anyway.

Between the lake and the street, the dilapidated structure I fantasized about living in when I was in elementary school isn't much to admire, just nostalgic and cool to me, and the gaggle of geese surrounding it, that seem not to mind their own green poo littering the grass beneath their webbed feet, race off the moment I pull up, squawking suspiciously as they waddle towards the water while I scan the lake and the twisting, dirt path that loops around it, following a pair on mountain bikes, both dressed in tight black shorts, tight shirts, no helmets. Aware that twelve laps equal a mile, I'm curious if they're conscious of that and biking a particular distance, or simply cycling and benefitting from the unexpected, improving weather, when I spot a retiree at the edge of the lake, hidden in a clump of trees roughly thirty feet away. Wearing a loose-fitting navy shirt, a bucket hat, and brown corduroy pants, he's in a folding chair with a fishing pole on his lap and an orange lunch box cooler next to him. There's a sign near him that reads **NO SKATING ON THIN ICE**, and, perfectly happy in his own, personal paradise, no work, no worries of the day, he sets his hands on his belly, stretches his legs, and watches the geese drift silently in a triangle formation while I circle the decaying building and peer inside a smeared window to see rickety furniture and tools dusty with cobwebs, the sight of the interior generating a chuckle out of me as I slightly shake my head at the humor in the silly, innocent thought process of a young kid and the things they concoct and say regarding a world they don't yet understand.

Hearing an animated cry of joy, I turn to find the old man's pole bent into an arch. Elated, he leaps from his seat, reeling it in steadily and supporting the pole with his body he brings the wriggling, silvery fish to his face, bursting with joy as it struggles on the line. "Oooh! Oooh!" he exclaims, trying gently to grab hold of the slippery body, eventually succeeding after several attempts. He unhooks the fish, kisses it on the lips, cracks another grin, whispers what I think is "Here ya go, fella," and tosses the fish back into the water. Plopping back down in his chair, he squirms to get comfortable, baits his rod, casts it, and this somehow stirs a childhood memory in me—I'm not positive how old I was, maybe ten, and I was sneaking through a corn field, with whom I can't recall, possibly a classmate, but a boy I sought to impress because I was carrying a BB gun—*We crept among the stalks, crouching, until we found a spot and knelt down low, the suspenseful minutes ticking by quietly as we waited in silence, searching the sky, an excited anticipation building in us, and just when we figured we were out of luck, while swapping mute, glum expressions to convey our disappointment, a small, yellow chick landed on the shriveled, brown kernels of an ear only a few feet from me, singing. Since I was closer, the nameless boy I don't remember tapped me on the shoulder, encouraging me, so I slowly raised the barrel, the tiny animal oblivious of the dire consequences of its innocent landing as it kept on chirping its lovely croon, and the gun kicked hard the moment I squeezed the trigger, my weak, scrawny chest quickly recoiling, but I hit my target, instantly ending the delicate, graceful bird's song, it's final sound a distressed bellow as it fell to the ground, landing on its back. I stared blankly at the gloppy red liquid mixing with the beautiful, golden feathers while the bird shivered briefly until it didn't, and I'd never felt so bad in my life.* I'm glad the fisherman still hasn't detected me because I'm not in the mood to exchange any type of salutation or conversation now, really, and wanting to be sure to avoid it, once I've gotten another satisfying view of the geese and the cottage I'd stopped to enjoy, as fulfilled as I can be, I continue on my way.

Worn copper flower baskets holding kaleidoscopic Petunias hang from black antique street lamps that line the oatmeal-colored sidewalks bordering the immaculate front lawns of affluent, brick and stone, slate-roofed mansions on Pomper Lane, a neighborhood I rarely enter—I have no reason to since I've never had a friend that lived here, or a relative, the sole reason I'd ever visited as an adult being to marvel at the properties I'd admired in my youth, but they'd struck me as so much grander back then, more palatial, the one with the marble lions guarding the entry to the driveway, the gothic, Victorian alone high atop the hill, the Spanish-style home that looked like it was misplaced, in the wrong country, its terra cotta clay roof so foreign to me at that age. It's pleasantly serene, quiet, the branches and leaves of the immense oak trees reaching over and across the road, casting shadows, and I wonder what the difference is in the prices of the intimidating estates now compared to back then, the fifteen-year gap seeming like an eternity as well as last week for the second time in less than an hour, re-

revealing the weird reality that 2038 is as far away as 2008, so to get *that* alarming, difficult-to-process fact out of my mind, for the seven minutes it takes me to make it to the next intersection, I imagine what it would be like to call one of these houses home, visualizing myself gazing through my bedroom window at night all tucked in my sheets during a snowstorm, a hot chocolate in my lap and a Christmas-themed movie playing while I admire the flakes as they fell from nothing, darkness, illuminated by the street lamp's amber lighting.

Braking to appreciate my favorite house here, the towering, skinny, white and beige Tudor that has the gigantic pot with elaborate carvings by the front door, I see a father, blue sleeves rolled to his elbows, tie undone, in the adjacent yard throwing a ball with his son, and, catching the kid's pitch bare-handed, he lobs it back gently but the boy completely misses it, losing his hat as he jumps in the air. The ball bounces into a row of hedges that separates their property and their neighbor's, and in his mad dash to retrieve it the boy almost trips before falling to his knees to scour the hedges on all fours. "That's okay! Nice try!" the dad shouts, peeking at his watch, tightening his tie, then buttoning his sleeves he notices me, nods, waves, turns back to his son. "Come here and give me a hug and a kiss! I have to go!" Forgetting the ball, his son twirls around, and smiling and sprinting with little coordination, all of his limbs flailing wildly, he drops his glove when he nears his dad, who, squatting, extends his arms and swoops him up, and this sweet, innocent exchange strikes a chord with me in regards to my lack of a significant male influence in my childhood—how I've never had a good father, coach, or teacher to admire, learn from, or educate me on things like how to tie a tie, unclog a sink, shave, change a tire, face challenges head on—a role model I could be grateful for who encouraged me, made me a better man, and now, feeling even more sullen and with a stop sign ahead, I stick my left arm straight down.

Approaching from my right as I'm biking halfway across the intersection, a woman in a white, Mercedes SUV runs the stop sign, veering in my direction, but brakes abruptly, lifting the rear end. "What the fuck, you idiot!?" she exclaims, leaning out the window, banging on the horn, before adding, "Fucking hurry up, asshole!" She takes a long pull from the green straw in her Starbucks cup before skimming her phone, which is in the same hand she's clutching the steering wheel with, prompting me to imagine her always answering it with a bored, bothered "hello" despite knowing who it is, and, well aware that nothing productive will result no matter how I address it, I choose not to acknowledge her, pedaling on, my indifferent attitude provoking the delightful lady with the unwarranted sense of self-entitlement to bolt into the intersection, screeching her tires as she swings a left while screaming several, parting obscenities at me I can't comprehend a final time.

The road is flat for as far as I can see, with no vehicles parked on it or driving my way, and that mixed with my slow speed persuades me to spontaneously remove my hands from my handlebars, stretching them into the air, a stunt I've never performed or considered attempting. After counting to twenty, I decide to shut my eyes and calmly count to three in my head, then five, before enthusiastically opening them and grasping the handlebars, and nowhere close to the edge of the road and unimpressed that something didn't happen, what, I'm not certain, I hop off and amble down the middle of Pomper towards the unique French Normandy-style house fifty feet ahead that resembles a small French castle, with its slate roof and brick narrowed in places by protruding mortar, giving the impression that it belongs in another country, another century, while surveying the yards to verify if anyone's on a nearby lawn, but I don't see anyone. Walking between the two BMWs in the driveway, I glance into the cracked window of the grey coupe, not the matching SUV, spotting a crumpled can on the passenger's seat, the spilt beer puddling the brown, leather interior, and the pavement wraps around to a patio, where I lay my cruiser against one of the rock pillars supporting the deck then meander through the tiki-themed bar, the TV below the selection of liquor bottles airing a sports news program. Introducing the highlights, a stout, balding, anchorman in a navy suit adjusts his striped tie, shifts in his chair. "You're with me, leather," he states as I scan the mulch bed bordering the cement patio for a rock to break one of the glass panels on the door. Noticing a strangely tinted stone, I pick it up, shake it, twist the fake bottom, only to realize there's no need for the key it contains when the knob isn't locked, so, I place the key back in its hiding place, tossing the rock in the vicinity of where I found it.

Poorly lit and with all the blinds drawn, his shady man cave's furnishings look like they were purchased at a yard sale with the intention of being ruined—the stained, ripped sofa and plaid recliner, the cheap coffee table, the scratched TV flanked by various mismatched pots on the mantle above the fireplace, six high, wooden stools strewn about, two flipped over, a neglected pool table with half-full glasses on its edges, balls scattered across the ripped green felt. Ignoring the kitchenette and bar in the corner and the entrance to the garage, I pause at the bottom of the stairs and cautiously unzip my backpack, then, after scribbling 10:02 and the number one and circling them in my diary, I fish out the handcuffs and taser and close the backpack just as quietly. On the second floor, to my right, there's a living room with a vaulted ceiling, three spinning fans hanging from it, leather furniture, and an immense TV mounted on a rock fireplace—it reeks of alcohol and stale cigarettes—and a kitchen to my left, where a large baggie filled with cocaine sits on the black marble counter between a toaster surrounded by crumbs and the dish filled sink, a slow drip leaking from the faucet, and unfazed by the white powder—I've never cared about or done drugs in my life—I make my way to the table in the dining area, pushing the dead, potted plant and pile of unopened mail and miscellaneous papers to the side to set down my backpack and the handcuffs, when I catch sight of a maroon blanket draped over the back of a wooden chair with "BHS Class of 2015" stitched into its fabric with gold thread, the familiar, ugly colors representing the local high school, which inexplicably triggers, of all things to opt for, memories of Valentine's Days over those four years, and I can picture first period being delayed so teachers could deliver roses purchased by boyfriends, girlfriends, or friends to teens thrilled to hear their names called, several students multiple times, to come to the front of class, me at my desk confident I'd remain seated.

Passing the home office that comes off as rarely used, with a messy desk holding a dusty computer and instructional stickers still attached to a tape-sealed filing cabinet, I take the next flight of stairs without exploring the rest of this level, grabbing the railing playfully so I can swing from it before lightly jogging to the top of the cushiony, carpeted steps, practically hopping each one, and, unsure whether to go right or left, I choose the former. The first room is empty with vacuum marks on the carpet and lit by an open window, the slight breeze inducing the dainty drapes to dance in the air, and through it I see two elderly women chatting in the neighboring backyard, one of them cradling a tan Pomeranian. The following room is full of stacked cardboard boxes labeled "Christmas," "Office," and "Summer," blocking the way to a half-bathroom, then when I reach the opposite end of the hall, there's a lone door.

I inch it open, relieved that it doesn't creak, and his bedroom is lit by what little sun is shining through the gap in the blinds as well as the monster TV that's attached to the foot of the bed, showing *The Long Kiss Goodnight*, the volume on mute. Hardly furnished, there's a dresser with three drawers pulled out, an artificial bamboo tree beside it, a nightstand on the other side of the bed, and the walls are a dark blue or green, I can't tell yet, no posters or art hanging on them, only framed photos of him—in a boat, on the beach, skiing, draped in a multitude of purple and yellow beaded necklaces in a crowd of people at Mardi Gras—and for no reason other than curiosity coupled with an unjustified confidence, I stroll around the mounted TV, avoiding a pair of jeans, boots, dirty boxers, and a sock on the linty, Persian rug, to look in the drawer that has a wad of cash, a bottle of cologne, a set of keys, and a pack of gum. Turning my attention to the tanned, muscular man under the sheets who's on his stomach and facing me, a line of drool dribbling from his contorted lips down his cheek and onto the pillow, I creep, tensely, closer to him, accidentally bumping into the nightstand, causing the remote on the edge that's touching a torn condom wrapper to teeter then fall. It hits the scant portion of the wooden flooring not blanketed by the enormous rug, creating the only sound I've made so far, at the worst possible moment, and when my excited, stupefied gaze shifts from the remote to him, his eyes flutter a few times before opening casually then widening immediately.

Sitting up promptly, he flings off the silk sheets, revealing he's naked. "What the fuck!?" he exclaims, wiping his chin, inspecting his hand. "Why are you in my—"

He attempts to leap out of his bed while shouting at me but I don't let him finish his sentence, jabbing his chest with the black taser, instantly sending his body into a radical convulsion as glops of drool spew out of his mouth and onto his chin, rendering his prior cleanup job pointless, and his thick arm that was grasping for me abruptly stops and falls with him when he slumps back onto the mattress, then, I stun him again, keeping my thumb on the button until I count to five to accommodate for his size and strength, while calmly saying "Mississippi" to myself between the numbers. IPPISSISSIM. In a bit of a daze, with my body swaying slightly in a small, circular motion, I stare at his partially shrouded, toned figure, not really eyeing or considering anything in particular, when he suddenly spasms, startling me in a way that convinces me he's going to make another move, so, out of reflex I zap him once more. I have no clue how long this will incapacitate him. Ten minutes? Thirty seconds? And, aware I won't do as well confronting him if I'm caught off guard a second time, and because it's the only thing I can think of that I know will definitively give me an advantage regardless of what might transpire, I snatch the razor blade that's lying across a line of cocaine on the magazine atop the table by the bed, jerk the sheets, which faintly smell of perfume, off his lower legs, finding the matching sock for the one on the floor on his right foot, and slit the Achilles on his left leg, precipitating a stringy spurt of blood to shoot in an arc like water from a fountain into the air, spraying his sheets and the wall. Gasping in pain, his young, husky body struggles to react, but his current, twitching state won't allow it; all he can muster is a garbled, distorted bellow, then again as the back of his skull smacks the floor with a hard thud when I yank him out of his bed, and visualizing this whole scene from above with the ceiling absent, like we're in one of those true crime TV shows and there's a camera shadowing us, I get a better grip on his wrists, continue pulling at his muscled arms, and lug him down the hall as he scarcely moans gibberish the entire time. Not troubling myself with lifting his torso when I haul him to the bottom of the stairs, his head bouncing comically off every step, I leave him by the front door, concealing the majority of an ornate, floral doormat I'm sure he didn't buy himself, then I search the level I'd regrettably neglected to investigate earlier, discovering a laundry room, a bedroom with clothes and towels spread on a twin bed, and his home gym. I flick the light on to find three mirrored walls, a brown and yellow plaid carpet, various dumbbells on a rack, a treadmill, a TV, speakers in all four corners of the ceiling, various trophies on wooden shelves, a water cooler, and, reminding myself that he could awaken at any moment, I half-jog to collect the handcuffs from the kitchen before returning to where I'd dropped him.

Still imagining us both from a loftier angle, I tow his hefty body against the wainscot paneling of the corridor towards the gym, his hips making it even tougher when they get caught in the doorway, forcing me to release his hands, step over him and align his legs so he's straighter, then, finally, I maneuver him into the room and, leaving him on his back, I pluck one of the towels from the pile next to the water cooler so I won't get bloody. I cuff his ankles to the supports of the steel weight rack that's aligned lengthwise with the only non-mirrored wall, fastening them tight, then slide two yellow 100lb kettle bells, so that he'll believe he'll have a chance to escape because of the limited movement, into place, above his head, securing his wrists to their handles, and stand to survey my work before getting dressed. Scrutinizing his muscled physique—zero fat, noticeable veins on his thick arms, defined abs—I wonder what type of regimen he follows for those type of results, certainly not one like the unvarying, daily exercise routine I've faithfully stuck to for years that obviously hasn't improved my appearance, only basically kept me the same, and this leads me into wondering what type of music he listens to while he's in here, or if he has a favorite song, which I deliberate about for longer than necessary, running through several titles and genres, eventually choosing to settle with rock or rap. No particular reason, simply an educated guess as to the type of music that might energize him during workouts, then, deciding I should get ready, I walk back to the kitchen, the faucet dripping steadily as I prepare, and even though its incessant plinking sound in the metal pan irritates me, I don't turn it off.

While slipping into the clear plastic coverall suit I recall the sweet, curly-haired old lady at the hardware store where I bought it last weekend, how I lied to her when she asked me what it was for, explained I was painting my den, and once I've tugged it so that it's not bunched up in my armpits and crotch and it now covers all my clothes underneath, I adjust the hood and elastic cuffs on the legs so that they shield my pants completely, slide on the aqua, rubber gloves I bought with everything else, snapping them tight, grab the goggles and hatchet from my backpack, then return to the gym, my thighs emitting a swishing noise with each stride. With him still comatose and no longer mumbling, I pair my phone with the Bluetooth hub below the photo of him flexing his biceps in a convertible Ferrari on a race track, increasing the volume until I can hear a loud, static filtering from the speakers, pull up the song on Spotify, wait a minute, then six, then eight, and after reading three of the golden plaques on his trophies that are for state high school football championships, years 2012, 2013, and 2014, and picturing myself owning a gym similar to this at home—watching TV while I jog on the treadmill, curling low weights on the bench and checking my posture in the mirrors—I impatiently revisit the kitchen to inspect the stainless steel fridge, spotting two bottles of water hidden by three Chinese takeout boxes with "thank you" and "enjoy" written on them in Asian-style red lettering, and curious what's in them because I love Chinese, preferring sweet and sour chicken and beef and broccoli, both with white rice, not brown, I take a peek, but when I unlatch the tiny metal bar whatever's inside is moldy and smells bad so I close it straightaway, and don't bother with the other two boxes.

Back in the gym I set one of the bottles in the cupholder on the treadmill so I can drink it at lunch because while searching the refrigerator I'd realized I'd forgotten to pack my Nalgene, then, uncapping the other, I tilt the bottle inch by inch, allowing a steady stream of water to spill on his handsome face, wetting his short, auburn hair. He comes to slowly at first, but starts shaking his head violently as I needlessly empty the rest of the bottle across his chest and chuck it as his face, bouncing if off his nose, then blinking briskly to try to get an understanding of what's going on, he frantically whips his head in my direction, his wild, nervous eyes scanning me up and down, worriedly conveying his wondering why I'm here and why I'm wearing what I'm wearing. He hasn't seen the axe yet.

"What the fuck?!" Hoisting his torso, his neck muscles straining, he adds, "What the fuck are you doing in my house, motherfucker?!", his deep voice resonating in the room as I nonchalantly slip the goggles over my eyes and tighten my hood, an exhilaration that I can't contain building in me, then, in an effort to stand, grimacing in a great deal of pain because of his sliced Achilles, he discovers that his wrists and ankles are cuffed. As much fun as this is to watch—I could do it all day knowing whatever he attempts won't matter—my exuberance is on the verge of exploding, I can't wait any longer, so I promptly produce the hatchet I've been hiding behind my back, the sight of it abruptly changing his demeanor to one of panic and dread. I press "play" and toss my phone on the floor as the beginning of Underoath's "Reinventing Your Exit" blasts through the speakers, inducing the kettle bell attached to his right arm, I'm assuming the stronger of the two, to rise, when, out of nowhere, I become wired, I see red, everything in this room covered in it—the treadmill and trophies and weights, the ceiling, pictures and mirrors—and, interpreting it as a foreboding cue, I bring the hatchet down hard on his shoulder. He wails this harrowing, ghastly squeal when his bones crack, the sound of them splintering unlike anything I've ever heard in my life, while blood spurts and flows from the lesion, splattering the mirrors and soaking the plaid carpet, but ignoring all of it with the word "INVINCIBLE" being shouted overhead, I gladly keep on swinging, amputating his limb after five whacks. With pink, purple, and crimson lacerated tissue hanging from the end of his arm as well as from his stubby shoulder, which is oozing mush, I remove the small box of salt from the pocket in my clear suit and pour it onto his gaping wound, immediately altering his cries to maniacal shrills, his face aquiver with fear as his frenzied eyes, which are bulging even more now, the irises and pupils almost absent, dash madly from his detached appendage to me, when I detect a pool of blood and bodily fluid spreading towards me, so before the expanding, gooey puddle underneath him can reach my shoes, I jump him with an unnecessary, added flair prompted by the music, seizing his left forearm. His eyes dart feverishly around the room, seeking what, I'm not sure, maybe a neglected weight on the floor or another unattainable object he believes can help, I guess, as a wild, panicked expression repeats in various forms on his twisted face while he gasps for air with heavy, ragged breaths, muttering unintelligible nonsense between his wild howls and sniveling, but I'm unable to comprehend what he's blabbering and I don't care, and I'm not certain why, but I decide that I want to chop off his leg instead of this arm, so I scoot down a foot or two with short hops, not out of necessity—I can easily get to it, more so just for fun—and swiftly plunge the hatchet into the upper part of his leg. Trembling severely and craning his neck, he elevates his head as best he can, his wild gaze shifting from his leg to the raised axe with chunks of his skin and muscle coated in blood clinging to the blade, then, dropping his head back down to the carpet he begins weeping in the way a sniffling boy would in the middle of a fit, which suddenly turns into a drooly, snotty sob, and our kerfuffle reminds me of the current state of the world, how individuals who hold opposing beliefs simply can't agree to disagree. I've always found it paltry and childish how a dispute of conflicting views concerning topics such as politics, religion, or minimum wage can divide society with such an immense mutual hatred, utter disdain, and it's ridiculous how people are somehow constantly getting offended until it goes on and on, building to a stage of absurdity, and why is it that most individuals seem to unfailingly retain an adamant opinion despite having zero wisdom or insight on the issue at hand, and hardly anyone can ever admit they're not educated enough about a subject to comment on it?

Choosing to forget about it, I revert my focus on what's in front of me, driving the silver blade down on his leg over and over, gore splashing my diaphanous suit, my khaki pants, shirt, and Members Only jacket untouched underneath. Twelve whacks. I sprinkle two pinches of salt on the exposed parts of his flesh and bone that are secreting liquids while he continues to bawl in horror, his sad look of desperation, which had visibly been worsening, instantly shifting to one of an absolute loss of hope as he stares at me like nothing in the world makes sense, but it doesn't faze me in any way, shape, or form, it's actually quite pleasing, so to respond to his pitiful countenance, I kick his useless leg under the weight rack. With that out of my way, I proceed to his other leg, chopping as vigorously and furiously as I can with a passion I wasn't aware I possessed, not paying the slightest bit of attention to his exasperated screeches, when I find myself wondering again what type of music he listened to while exercising in here, whether or not he has a favorite song, and with me now humming to the deafening lyrics filling the room, he glances wearily, vacantly, to his left, into the mirror that reflects us—catching my ensanguined, thin-plastic encased figure kneeling beside him, spews of his blood flying everywhere, spraying his equipment and the weight rack—prior to blubbering one, weak, final scream as I separate his second leg. Thirteen. I have no idea why it took an additional swing, but I don't get the reaction I'd anticipated, that had previously amused me, when I dash salt on this stub, and, turning to see his sporadically fluttering eyes fixated on the ceiling, registering nothing, I wonder if he's bled to death or lost consciousness, grinning and chuckling at this lack of knowledge, then, standing to get to his lone, remaining limb, I notice the two women outside the window still talking on the lawn, the room's thin white curtains, though drawn, permitting me to witness their discontent with the loud music emanating from here. Annoyed, the lady wearing golf attire points to her ears as her neighbor struggles to cradle the pet that's wriggling in her arms, the pair shaking their heads in unison until the small, fluffy dog predictably escapes, scurrying further across the yard, forcing the women to dart off chasing it, waving their hands wildly in the air. Considering it odd and kind of neat that I can see them but they can't see me and what I'm doing, I move on to his left arm, severing it with elated chops, as steadfastly as when I began, then, after tallying it all up and concluding that it took thirty-five whacks to relieve him of his four appendages, I take my last swing, burying the hatchet into the carpet next to his expressionless face, the wooden handle angled and aimed at the ceiling, and, for the first time ever, he doesn't have a single word to say to me.

As soon as I kill the music, flashes of gold and maroon hues all at once begin to flicker and pulse everywhere as I look around the room while various, endured, helpless images of past-lived, grim years spontaneously materialize out of thin air between the jumbled, dual-colored arrangements, and realizing that I'm breathing rather heavily, I concentrate on the floor for a few moments, but unable to stop the rush of colors, I put my hands on my hips, then on the top of my head, my chest heaving, so I inhale slowly and deeply through my nose, pause, exhale calmly from my mouth, and repeat. Catching a glimpse of myself in the mirror, my goggles crooked, blood dripping from my gloves, my hair slightly tousled despite my usual morning maintenance to avoid such an ordeal, my face is unrecognizable, giving me the feeling that I'm peering into the eyes of a stranger, so I spin around awkwardly and check the mirror, but it doesn't improve my condition, and after peeling the gloves off I need to twirl myself five more times while vigorously rubbing the phosphenes out of my eyes before the graphic delusions disappear and I finally recognize myself. I tilt my head, scrunch my lips, and neither the colors or images appear again, the sense of complete abundant despair they'd brought on dissipating with them, so I slide the goggles off my head, flinging them in the direction of the trash can in the corner, missing, which baffles me because it's only three feet away, and, reminding myself to be mindful of not staining my pants or shoes or socks when I disrobe, I unzip the suit.

Like a ghastly Halloween display you'd encounter in a haunted house, or a victim in a horror movie whose sole intention is to disturb you, his gaping, messy wounds resemble pure gore, a bloody discharge seeping from each stub and all of his limbs, his right leg the only one scarcely clinging on, not by bone or muscle, but by skinny threads of tendons and skin, including a glistening, meaty chunk I missed at the bottom, but I don't stress it, it's a trivial detail at this point, and his head, now remarkably pale and glazed with saliva and tears, lies in a slanted position so that his expired eyes are staring at me, his mouth frozen open, as I lick my palms, then flatten and neatly arrange my disheveled curls. Once I'm pleased with my appearance, I kneel close to him, our gazes locking, with nothing of significance running through my mind until I question who will find him—a friend popping in to exercise? A girl he's been dating? His parents? I imagine them all at the front door, suspicious of their unanswered knocks, perhaps deeming it strange, but not fearing the worst when they enter and call his name while wandering the house, oblivious to the fact that they'll be *that person* in a headline, the subject of a story on TV everyone believes and trusts only befalls somebody else, and I envision his best friend who's also handsome and in excellent shape, stopping in his tracks and backpedaling through the doorway into the hallway's opposite wall; then, an attractive woman with blonde hair—no, chestnut— losing hold of her phone as she emits a petrified shriek and covers her shuddering lips prior to sprinting onto the lawn, screaming; lastly, his parents being enveloped in shock, terror, and panic, his mother forced to buckle at her knees and clutch her spouse for support before struggling to reach her son in a fit of hysteria as her husband holds her back. I picture all of their mouths agape when they encounter an atrocity they presumed would be the last thing they could have ever expected to witness today, then, while gathering my stuff, I imagine him miraculously surviving this and becoming the star of his own reality show, going so far as to invent comical and silly scenarios for him to perform in addition to confronting menial daily tasks in the state he's in—preparing meals, washing dishes, cleaning the house, tending to a pet, canned laughter playing whenever he topples over or fails—and with all of that consuming my thoughts, most importantly, I still can't help but wonder what his favorite workout song was.

When I step out onto the patio, I'm surprised to see a significantly clearer sky, and while walking my bike past the BMWs, paying no interest to the spilt beer I know is there, I realize that whoever stumbles across his dismembered body could possibly hear and turn off the kitchen faucet beforehand, which piques my curiosity as to what else they might learn about how he lived, hidden details about his life he wouldn't care for certain acquaintances or family members to chance upon—the cocaine, the disastrous kitchen, the dirty boxers and clothes on the bedroom rug, porn, an unacceptable bathroom in terms of cleanliness and sanitation—before I ask myself whether I should have turned the water off. It would have been the responsible thing to do. I'd have done it anywhere else. But by the time I'm at the end of the driveway I've determined that I don't owe him anything. Anything at all. Not even that.

Down the street and around the corner, two young girls, maybe eight or nine, in summer dresses, one teal, the other purple, are on all fours on the sidewalk, tongues out, bright chalk in their fingers, the bucket on the ground near them crammed with a rainbow of sticks. "Finished!" the girl in the teal dress exclaims, high-fiving her playmate, who stands, clasps her hand and helps her up. Not bothering with the bucket, they drop their chalk and admire their artistry, a hopscotch board made of various, colored squares – orange, yellow, green, pink... There are ten squares, and the girl in the purple dress jumps first, springing from box to box, separating and closing her legs, adding a twirl, singing lyrics to a song I'm not familiar with, her friend in tune, cheering her on. "Nice, Sophie! Yeah!" she shouts. Once the girl whose name I haven't learned takes her turn, they notice me, but it doesn't deter their singing as they simultaneously look to each other, nod in agreement, and, with toothless smiles, wave for me to join them while squealing, "Come on!" before reverting right to their song.

Grinning, I hop off my bike and release my grip on my handlebars, forgoing the kickstand, a move I exclusively make on grass, letting the bike crash to the asphalt, and jogging over to the girls they nudge me from behind, not aggressively, reassuringly, towards the squares, so I jump onto the first square, the second, the third, while they start clapping faster for me, emphatically cheering and singing the song I don't know, then, after circling back and seeing their gleeful faces encouraging me to take another turn, I go again, quickening my pace and flailing my arms through the air as a neighbor mowing his lawn in a sweat-stained brown collared shirt removes his hat to wipe his forehead while eyeballing me oddly, and when I'm done the girls slap my palm before kneeling indifferently to pluck two sticks of charcoal chalk out of the bucket between them. Reminiscent of the old man at the lake and how happy he was in his own little paradise, and the woman on her balcony in the alley, these ecstatic girls have suddenly made me aware that everybody has their own type of paradise, their own definition of it—an island surrounded by a brilliant, blue sea to swim in, working a job that you love, being in the mountains, motherhood—and, picking up my bike, I give each girl her own individual wave, but they're oblivious, too busy drawing black birds shaped like Ms, lots of them, on the oatmeal sidewalk, so I pedal off humming a tune similar to whatever it was they were singing.

iridescent – adjective : showing luminous colors that seem to change when seen from different angles **wytai** – noun : a feature of modern civilization that suddenly strikes you as absurd and grotesque **bombinate** – verb : buzz, hum **keta** – noun : a random image from your distant past that leaps back into your attention **gossamer** – noun : a fine, filmy substance consisting of cobwebs spun by small spiders **dracula monkey orchid** – noun : an epiphytic orchid originally described in the genus Masdevallia, but later moved to the genus, Dracula; in most instances represents death and evil and darkness **idyllic** – adjective : extremely happy, peaceful, or picturesque **alimono** – **mia** – noun : the fear that learning the name of something – a bird, a constellation, an attractive stranger – will somehow ruin it

HCTOCSPOH. LAST NIGHT I'D PLANNED the best route to travel, mapping out my course and deciding on the order of my stops after dinner, a late-night talk show playing in the background where the host was quizzing pedestrians in the city with questions, such as "What galaxy are we in? Can you name all seven continents? Which one are we on? What century are we in?" Most of the participants didn't know the answers to any of them, several of the teens uttered contemplative "hmmms" while laughing at themselves, their deficiency in basic facts; a pale guy with long, greasy hair that hung in his face, after staring blankly into the camera and saying nothing for what seemed like minutes, responded "California?," as if he were asking, when questioned with "What is the capital of the United States?"; and, after being given a hint related to our galaxy, that it shared its name with a popular candy bar, everyone replied with "Mars." However, when the same interviewees were asked to identify three of the Kardashians, four of the cities the *Real House Wives* series is filmed in, or the location of the ongoing celebrity domestic abuse trial, they answered rapidly and confidently, peppering their answers with additional, perceptive, insightful tidbits of information to further prove that if they weren't educated on the subject matter of the former test, they were certainly well-schooled in the latter.

At first, I had settled on a different route as opposed to the one I ultimately ended up choosing for today, one that was 8.1 miles shorter, saving me roughly forty-eight minutes, assuming my average speed was ten miles per hour, but in the original route the comic book shop was the fifth destination, and the thought of carrying and balancing that heavy cardboard box for longer than necessary wasn't feasible, nor was the idea of it getting wet if it were to rain later. I'd lose time, but I wasn't able to calculate how much exactly, so I determined that even if it did cost me twenty or thirty minutes, ridding myself of the box sooner than later was the best course, not to mention that spilling its contents due to the greater probability of an accident caused by unforeseen circumstances or extraneous variables would definitely be a terrible situation.

With my next appointment merely 3.12 miles away, I pedal and coast, pedal and coast, in no real rush so that I can enjoy what is anything but a normal bike ride, I suppose because of my elevated mood brought on by the elderly lady on her balcony, the fishing senior at the lake, the girls on the sidewalk, maybe also realizing what paradise really is, and for some reason I decide to steer onto Woodstock Circle, a street that reconnects to the one I'm currently on, my cruiser continuing to squeak as I easily conquer a moderate hill, then drift down the other side while recalling those two girls and how nice they were to me, wishing there was an ice cream truck or lemonade stand there, so that I could reciprocate their goodwill with a kind act, but I don't let it trouble me, especially since I didn't bring my five dollars with me, anyway, and when I return to Hickory, I'm in the mood to circle Woodstock again despite having no clue how many hours, possibly minutes, are at my disposal, so I swing left and then, once I've climbed the easy hill a second time, I stop for three deer crossing. They glance at me skittishly while traipsing hesitantly across the street, the clicks of their hooves on the asphalt odd to their inexperienced ears, before bolting off the moment they hit the grass, casually and fluidly hurdling a fence twice their size to disappear into the woods, and, not far ahead, where Woodstock starts to dip, a bearded guy in his twenties with a stunted body and no neck whizzes out of his driveway in an electric wheelchair. Spinning a one-eighty he checks his mailbox, his shoulders drooping when he finds it empty, then, steering the toggle stick on the arm, he zooms back up the paved drive only to brake abruptly as he pulls up next to the electric lift of a van that's idling near the closing garage door, a blue and white handicap parking permit hanging from the rearview mirror, before a Hispanic woman wearing a striped sweater that's swallowing her shuts the sliding door behind him, then half-jogs around the front of the van, a purse dangling from her elbow, to hop into the driver's seat. It's so disheartening for me to see a person forced to endure a life of dependence on a chair to get from place to place, hired nurses to assist with day-to-day affairs, special ramps to access an entrance. Most people never think about it, taking their health for granted. It's not until you're sick, laid up, or broken that you truly appreciate it—the ability to run and jump, skip, sit Indian-style, use the stairs, ride a bike, hike a trail whenever you want—and I imagine that if by some miracle this young man were able to stand out of his seat right now, he'd sprint wildly across his lawn with deer-like strides, howling shouts of joy.

Cycling leisurely and expending whatever mindless energy is required to keep moving forward, I blankly glimpse at the yards and trees and houses as a dog barks at me from its patio, not perceiving even a fraction of it, all of it blurring together, when, without warning, I'm not sure why, maybe because of the immature deer, or perhaps the handicap parking permit that awakened memories of my grandfather who died a decade ago, but random images from my childhood begin popping up in my head, a few pleasant, others not so much, slipping by one after another like movie clips, each transiently grabbing my interest and curiosity, enticing me to attempt to capture a sense of the chain of events around what I'm viewing, what else transpired, was said and took place, but I can't and the short films play out reel by reel: I'm ten on a cold Christmas, the first holiday we'd ever celebrated downstairs, in our new den with wood-paneled walls, the upright piano mom won at a church raffle in the corner, wrapping paper cluttering the floor, my father lounging in his La-Z-Boy the entire day, sulking and drinking, not speaking a word, my mom and I eating breakfast by ourselves; it's instantly sunny, and I'm twelve and sitting in the front seat of a bus by myself travelling with my church youth group on my first trip to Busch Gardens, and I curl my hand into a fist and pump my arm, smiling when the eighteen wheeler passing us honks, everything inside the park—the trees, the attractions, and the European buildings—is so colorful and vivid to my preteen psyche, happy noise surrounds me, cheerful screams and yells, I'm not tall enough for the roller coasters; now it's summer and I'm at Frobisher Lake, I'm thirteen, boats are gathered in the water below, loud music blaring from the green yacht filled with drinking partiers, there's a rope swing that throws you twenty feet above the water that I'm too scared to try, boys egg me on to stop stalling and go, ridicule me when I hesitate and can't, before I mope back down the path alone; it's Fall, I'm maybe eleven, or twelve, and in my yard, the tall grass that needs to be cut is scattered with leaves and there's a scaly, slithery, black snake underneath the porch, it hisses at me and curls up to strike while I—; I'm in eighth grade and Fred, the friendly old janitor with a wrinkled, tanned face and kind eyes who always wore a navy trucker cap waves to me as he approaches me in the student-filled hallway wheeling a large, grey garbage can; now I'm in home ec in middle school, an elective I'd picked in lieu of band, physical education, and theatre, there's uneven sewing, so stuffing spills out of the open portions of the misshapen, baseball glove pillow in my hand, coating my desk, littering the floor; now I'm building my first bike jump with a neighbor in his yard out of nine-inch metal car ramps, we fly into the air, the boy I'm with whose name I can't remember stacks one on top of the other before zooming down the hill on his BMX to launch himself off the unstable ramp, but I don't see what happens because—; I'm wearing a red Lacoste shirt at a birthday party for Michael, a classmate who lived nearby, there's a contest and we have three minutes to mold anything we choose out of a stick of pale white gum for a prize, when I'm done I proudly display my dog on his small, cardboard stand, but I get last place, and the kids ignore my attempts to interact until they choose to mock me incessantly and the parents let them, so, dejected, I walk back home alone early wondering why I was invited; in a flash, I've lost an incisor at dinner chomping on an ear of corn, I run my tongue along the smooth gum as I gaze into the mirror, and I wrap the tooth in toilet paper to put under my pillow for a silver dollar when I awaken; now it's sunny and windy and I'm in the woods behind our house climbing on a pile of discarded lumber my mom advised me to avoid, a rusty nail pierces my shoe so we go to the hospital where I get a shot and cry; JoJo, my hamster, plays in his orange hideout among wood chips as I fall asleep and then wake up the next morning to find him dead and stiff in his cage, stuck between his house and silver metal bars; it's Saturday morning and cartoons are starting soon, so I rise at dawn and fix a bowl of cereal, plop on the floor three feet directly across from the TV to watch Tom & Jerry, Scooby Doo; I'm ascending a tree, the ground getting further and further away, the twenty feet so much more intimidating from this height than from below; now back indoors I wait for the ice cream truck and, unable to see it, I can hear the sweet melody it echoes, so I rush out my front door with a dollar in my hand, hoping it won't pass before I reach it; it's my first time staying awake for New Year's Eve, there's ribbons, confetti, people in funny hats kiss at the end of a count down, I fight falling asleep to feel grown up; I'm at Trelawny campground, bundled up in my sleeping bag and looking up at the stars, it's chilly but the enticing allure of a campfire at night as it crackles eclipses the cold; all of a sudden mom's singing Elvis songs in the kitchen while I'm building forts and castles in the living room, blankets are strewn over and across chairs that lie on their sides, and I'm hiding in my fort, no adults allowed; lastly I'm at a pool, David wraps his arms around me and jumps into the deep end, embracing me while I kick and flail, struggling to escape, but I can't as I watch the distorted world from under the water.

Passing Pine, Willard, and Wyndhurst, I stop at an intersection, swing a left, and now I'm on Wellington, which merges with Lakewood, an area of this city that's also quite nice, but a lot newer, built five years ago on what used to be a vast field, most of the homes remarkably similar, separated by easy, general subtleties such as a variation in the color of brick or driveways and garages on opposite sides of the house, promptly erected residences that lack the precision, attention to detail, and craftsmanship of the ones in the preceding suburb—cookie cutter, interchangeable—like you could mix and position them however you fancied without being able to tell the difference. A green garbage truck ahead of me with a couple of men riding footholds on the rear decelerates so they can jump off, and after emptying four bins into the truck, they jog to the adjacent yard, do the same, hop back on, turn onto Vine, and, pleased the day ended up the way it did, the idea of running these errands in a downpour and constantly wiping my glasses while trudging through soggy conditions from one stop to the next seeming awful, I look up with appreciation at the beautiful sky, enjoying the sun on my face all the way to Montoya Drive.

With no more homes over the next quarter mile, the empty lots for sale become forest and the paved road turns to thin gravel shaded by the surrounding trees, eventually ending in a cul-de-sac where a dark olive log cabin sits alone. Matching the forest surrounding it perfectly, it effortlessly blends in, creating the impression that it's a natural part of the landscape, as if it's supposed to be there, nestled in nature far from the commercial, stale aura of the rest of the neighborhood. Verdant ivy creeps and winds up the cabin's exterior and its rock chimney, onto and spanning the roof; red roses twist their thorny stems and petals in and out of a maroon, latticed fence that spans the front, going around and above the windows and the mustard door that has a stone pathway lined with miniature bowls overflowing with mahogany marigolds leading from it to the mailbox; and the grass is lush and a vibrant green, cut in a checkered pattern that's reminiscent of a baseball field, the edges bordering the pruned boxwoods that provide a perfect boundary between his lawn and the woods. A mustard-colored fence and a row of enormous cherry blossom trees perpendicular to the boxwoods obstruct the view of the backyard, and, for no particular reason, I lean my cruiser against the telephone pole as opposed to taking it to the driveway, undo my pant leg, and remove my helmet. Ambling a few feet in the wet grass prior to crossing the street, I slide off my backpack, grab my notebook, scribble the time, the number one, circle them, and then, because I forgot to earlier, it was probably the hopscotch that distracted me, I slap down a massive, sloppy "X," marking my previous entry complete. Strolling by the front door without testing it, I glance at it twice to confirm that the strange, bronze knocker resembling a boar's head is actually in the shape of a boar's head, not a pig's, and it is, and it seems oddly ugly to me, like it doesn't belong, then, fingering the handle of the gate to the right of the house, I pause to peek behind me to double check, but there's no need, nobody's around, as a matter of fact it's eerily quiet, so I push on the ivy-covered door.

The gate emits a slow, continuous squeak with every inch as I open it enough to squeeze sideways and under the wreathed archway to a hidden backyard that is immaculate—I can't help but be impressed—the hidden utopia of luscious pigments impelling me to gaze in awe as if I'm admiring a marvelous painting in a museum, with a pair of amazingly golden ginkgo trees flanking me, two bright blue Chinese wisterias in the opposite corners, purple and pink hydrangeas lined among them perfectly outlining a manicured lawn cut in the same pattern as the front, and a garden full of various, blossoming flowers and plants. In the middle of the garden, which is etched out to occupy exactly half the backyard, a man old enough to be my father, wearing a horrendous, orange patterned shirt and plaid pants, is watering the greenery surrounding him with his back to me, and, deciding I'm no longer a museumgoer, my prepossessing surroundings become a backdrop as I stride towards him, the sounds of soothing, inharmonic chimes filling the air while he turns slowly in my direction, raising the hose that I now see has a MiracleGro feeder attached to it and aiming the arc of turquoise water at the next row of flowers, but instead of reaching for the taser in my backpack, I casually scoop up the shovel that's standing conveniently at the edge of the garden to my right, its blade buried in the soil. Still concentrating on his current task, he notices me but doesn't react as I expected, or even flinch. Instead, a glimpse of peculiarity is all I get from his squinting eyes, then bewilderment as he furrows his brow and cocks his head slightly, and, refusing to give him time to respond, I lift the shovel I've been dragging for several feet off the ground to swing at his cheek, and I don't like the sharp, weird sound it makes, but when the hose that was in his hand sprays everywhere, briefly showering both of us, I forget this, then as he collapses to the dirt, his idyllic world of solitude and tranquility shattered, the only things I can sympathize with are the delicate irises being squashed beneath him, and I wince. All of this provokes some birds that were nesting on a nearby branch to fly off in a flash, and when I jerk my head back to crack my neck it won't at first, so I do it two more times until it does, then toss the shovel on top of his chest.

Involuntarily picturing him being younger than he is now, I visualize what his appearance would have looked like years ago—blonde hair and a goatee, a slimmer waist, sans glasses—which stirs up a fuzzy mental image of lengthy hallways lined with rows of lockers in between classroo— Bryan! The name of the boy whose backyard I built the ramp in pops in my brain, prompted by his association with my present thoughts, the thoughts that I now choose to forget, returning the guy in front of me to his present age, reminding me instantly of what I'm here to do, and to confirm that I've acknowledged this, I actually nod in recognition before sliding off my bag, then jacket, to calmly fold the latter and place at the edge of the garden.

With blood and bits of his hair stuck to the end of the blade, I begin digging up the soft soil bordering the Dracula monkey orchids as numerous bees bombinate in the air around us, flying from plant to plant, and, aware this would have been a significantly slower and more daunting chore had it not rained so much, I gratefully pace my scoops, averaging two per ten seconds, pausing for thirty seconds to recuperate every five minutes, when, on my eleventh break, I hear an indistinct rustle followed by a moan, so I grab the taser out of my backpack and shock him longer than necessary, driving and twisting the device into his balls. He spasms as his body locks up, and his head, that's bleeding and swelling on the right side, shakes violently, splattering his face with specks of blood from the stream that's flowing out of the cut on his temple and dripping off his ear, down his neck, and I electrocute him in his balls once more for no other reason than—just because—holding the taser for a count of four while wondering what's running through his mind—if he's scared, angry, confused—but watching him lie there, his eyes rolling into the back of his head as he twitches uncontrollably with his arms pinned to his chest, his wrists and hands bent and dangling like a squirrel, I happily conclude that he's thinking nothing, and I return to digging. The pile behind me gradually becomes wider and taller, the hole I'm standing in deeper and deeper, it's almost waist high now, and, while I'm wiping my brow during another brief rest, the Sun emerges fully from the clouds, its beams penetrating the pink branches of the tress that hide the yard, creating an exquisite array of chaotic, iridescent patches and luminous hues and rays that blend magnificently into the already brilliant garden, setting a stunning stage for me to resume my work on. Whatever fatigue I was enduring is gone, my energy restored by the inconceivable natural beauty encompassing me, encouraging me to persist with more diligence but less exertion as I chuck shovel loads onto neat piles to my left in a smooth rhythm, surprisingly sweating less, when this ubiquitous kaleidoscope of color unexpectedly strikes a chord from my past, what, I'm unclear on, maybe a scene in a movie, a cartoon I saw as a kid, a page in one of my comic books, or possibly a forgotten event in my life, but I opt not to find its origin now that I've convinced myself that if I do it will somehow ruin this moment, and for the thirty minutes it requires to complete the hole, I unintentionally hum "Call on Me" by Eric Prydz for the last fifteen.

Finished, I'm thankful that I paced myself, and even though I'm sweating, and despite everything I've just done,

I'm not too tired, so, jumping out of the hole, I stab him with the taser again to guarantee he remains the way he is, then, not sure I need it or have the time to spare, I decide to spend a few minutes recovering, not in the bubble swing hanging from the wisteria because the swaying sensation might make me nauseous, but in one of the black, metal chairs in the shady corner under the other wisteria, and, relaxing as best I can, I stretch my legs and steal a sip of the lemonade from the mason jar on the table next to me, which is quite good. Setting the sweating jar down, I let six or seven minutes tick by, then, as if it were meant to be, some sort of cosmic connection between me and nature at this moment, with the amazing spectrum continuing to radiate around me, the blue leaves of the Chinese wisteria above me so intense, a honey bee lands on my forearm, moseying and buzzing its way to my wrist, evoking memories of my grandfather—us at the lake on my tenth birthday, and there was a bee on my skinny white thigh and he told me it wouldn't sting me if I let it be, so I did—and I do so now, but I must not be that interesting because it doesn't stay long, leaving as suddenly as it came, hovering away and vanishing among the purple and blue Hydrangeas bushes beside me.

Countless gossamer threads hang, dancing in the gentle breeze, from the Alberta dwarf spruces branches I ease by so as not to disturb them or the tulips at the edge of the garden, both wet from either last night's shower or the watering I abruptly stopped earlier, and, kneeling, I blindly count and take six zip ties out of my bag while scanning the dwarf spruce closest to me for spider mites, an old habit I had when I grew these tiny trees, but since they're impossible to see without a magnifying glass, I don't give it much effort.

Rotating the spasming man onto his stomach, I'm careful not to disrupt the surrounding vegetation, doing my best to move him minimally so that I can secure his legs and wrists, using two zip ties for the former, four for the latter, and satisfied that he won't be able free himself, I flip him into his grave, ensuring that he lands on his back when I do, snag the duct tape, tear off a strip, and slap it across his quivering mouth. The thin, coiled 36-inch tube and pocket knife I cut out of their packaging yesterday so I wouldn't have to do it this morning or deal with it presently are in the front pocket of my backpack, and once I've sliced a small hole in the tape on his mouth, I insert the tube down his throat. Still kneeling, I look over my shoulder at the goofy faces of the Dracula monkey orchids, **SDIHCRO YEKNOM ALUCARD**, which are fixated on me, laughing, in pursuit of my attention, so, deeming that they've warranted it, I spin on my toes with my elbows on my knees to balance myself while happily recollecting my favorite course in high school, horticulture—the reason I can identify each plant, bush, and tree in this yard—and, humorously glaring back at them, my smirk grows wider, marginally revealing my teeth, all of this eventually eliciting an unexpected chuckle from me, and with that I stand and seize the shovel.

Ignoring his muffled murmurs, I grab my notebook, and leaning the shovel's wooden handle against my chest, I hastily mark an X where it's supposed to be before flipping to a blank piece of paper, scribbling three words, ripping the page out, crumpling it into a ball, and tossing it in the pit near his bloated, hemorrhaging head, the side I struck now ballooned to the point that he temporarily reminds me of Frankenstein, then, with the way he's positioned and his circumstances—wrists bound behind him, feet restricted, lying in this hole—of a mobster who's violated an unforgivable mafia rule and is being buried for retribution in the middle of a corn field, in a film or TV show.

Unconcerned with pacing myself like before, I throw in shovel upon shovel of dirt on top of and around him while adjusting the tube, his convulsing body gradually disappearing, trapped under wet dirt and mud with nowhere to go, no hope of escaping, his pitiful, distressed murmurs growing quieter and quieter, when, probably because of the laughing monkeys and his sudden, confined predicament, I start thinking about zoos, not one in particular, but the silly idea of them—poor animals that should be freely roaming their native spaces in the wild, instead caged in an unfamiliar environment, stared and gawked at on a daily basis by strangers who stuff food into their mouths, sip on sodas, snap family photos and selfies, all the while laughing and enjoying themselves, and by the time I've finished the pit and I'm circling it filling in shallow spots and shifting dirt, a number of ridiculous, farcical trademarks of contemporary society, several absurd or sad, others normal, everyday occurrences, have popped into my head—from the concept of life insurance to busy fathers too invested in their jobs, earning money for their families but too busy to even find an evening to spend quality time with them, to complex materialistic work-driven lives and mankind's attachment to electronic devices, to feigned social media personas racking up thousands of friends online, but nobody to share true joy with, to how most people are willing and eager to judge, alarmed and agitated when judged, to how we're all connected yet so isolated, neighbors in dense urban areas unacquainted with one another, to how we never cherish the present, always craving and anticipating what's to come, to purchasing unnecessary clothes, automobiles, and appliances in order to impress others or fleetingly feel better about ourselves, to selfies at the edge of a cliff on a mountain trail despite the danger, to knowing the prices of cars, big-screen TVs, computers, and phones, but the value of nothing, to how humanity yearns for sedation in lieu of invigoration, to greedy consumerism, to, arbitrarily, being afraid of insects, yet willing to dart through traffic crowded with two-ton vehicles, to the unrealness of our unlimited access to and ability to eat almost any food anywhere at any restaurant, to how certain religions and individuals *truly* believe God only made a fraction of us and will exclusively embrace that small percentage upon death, to people having time for everything except people, to sleep becoming a longing, to society's "entertain me now or I'm leaving, you've got five seconds" mentality, to entitlement, to the health care system, to the break-neck pace we live our life in, the rage that reveals itself over anything that slows it down. Once I've flattened and leveled the ground as best I can so that it's smooth and I'm pleased with how his grave looks, I straighten the tube, snatch up a handful of soil and let the grains of dirt slowly filter out of my clenched fist, spilling into the tiny hole, doing it twice more until it's overflowing, leaking soil, then, chucking the shovel and not bothering to see where it lands, I dismiss the grave I recently dug and filled and the sneering monkeys, giving neither the slightest departing glance as I stroll nonchalantly to the edge of the garden, slide on my jacket, pick up my backpack, and, stealing an appreciative final glimpse of the menagerie of pigments and flowers and idyllic beauty I've been experiencing, I unlatch the mustard gate without worrying about its squeaking or needing to turn sideways like earlier when I kick the door open and back out under the ivy.

The air is noticeably hotter on the street, out of the shade, the Sun exceedingly brighter than when I arrived, and, after checking my phone and barely registering a text advertising gutters and a phone call I missed almost an hour ago from an eight-seven-seven number, I wonder why I didn't switch it to silent the instant I place it back in my pocket, but I don't bother in case of I don't know what, and deciding to walk my bike to the path in the woods instead of hopping on, I happily visualize that aged gardener's futile attempts to escape the suffocating wet mud and soil in all that darkness, his afternoon plans, which most likely included sipping on lemonade in one of those metal chairs and admiring his years of sweat and dedication, laid to waste. I read an article in a magazine last month while waiting for a haircut that listed the major regrets people had when they were older, like not travelling enough and feeling they weren't true to themselves or honest with people, that they'd wasted an excessive amount of time worrying while squandering decades comparing themselves to others and being discontented with what they already had, or they wished they had opted to work less and put more of a concerted effort into pursuits they repeatedly pushed off to a tomorrow that never came, and taken additional risks with the hope of success versus avoiding them for fear of failure, but mostly they wished they had possessed the courage to express their feelings, kept in touch with friends, told the people dear to them how much they loved them, and, lastly, that they'd allowed themselves to be happier by appreciating the world around them, its beauty, chosen to live more in the moment—ultimately that they had a second chance. But I don't care at all what this man thought, what his feelings were, if he regretted any of his choices, or felt as if he missed out on something, just how nice it'd be for the meteorologists to continue being wrong about the forecast for the rest of the day, for it to be radiant and shiny until the Sun disappears, then, wondering if it really matters anymore as long as it doesn't rain, I promptly reject this ridiculous idea, deciding it does, it absolutely does.

sonder - noun : the awareness that everyone has a story, that everyone is living a life as vivid and complex as your own picturesque - adjective : visually attractive, especially in a quaint or pretty style onism – noun : the awareness of how little of the world you will experience ambedo – noun : a kind of melancholic trance in which you become completely absorbed in vivid sensory details - raindrops skittering down a window, tall trees leaning in the wind mahplohanzia – noun : the frustration of knowing how of being unable to fly, unable to stretch out your arms and vault into the air middling – noun : the tranquil pleasure of being near a gathering but not quite in it mimeomia – noun : the frustration of knowing how neatly you embody a certain stereotype monachopsis – noun : the subtle but persistent feeling of being out of place zysy – noun : a conjuction or opposition, especially of the moon with the sun harmonoia – noun : an itchy sense of dread when life feels just a hint too peaceful / vellichor – noun : the ethereal feeling of looking down at the world through an airplane window, able to catch a glimpse of far-flung places you'd never see in person

THE WOODED AREA NEXT TO the cabin has miles of wandering trails with numerous intersections and a variety of ways to roam, a constant loop you could stay lost in if you didn't know where you were going, and I don't picture myself from above like I did this morning because I wouldn't be able to see myself through the branches and leaves of the trees, anyway, and, after circumventing a small log that hasn't yet been split and removed by the crew that maintains the trails, I ride up and down the roller coaster-like section meant for mountain bikers slowly and steadily because I'm not good at this part, plus my cruiser isn't built for it, all the while attempting not to concern myself with accuracy or minutes as I merely try to enjoy the trail, following the trees periodically marked with maroon paint slashes, that wind around a corner, down a slope, then past a cluster of huge boulders and a burnt-out firepit that teenagers use as a drinking spot, cans and bottles littering the dirt, but soon, even though I don't want to, I remind myself anyway that it's 4.04 miles to my destination, and there's no reason I go with this undesired decision other than because I always have. Arriving at an intersection, I briefly get the idea of steering left onto a different path with yellow-marked trees leading to the rope bridge that crosses a decent-sized creek, a location I'm particularly partial to, but with zero deliberation I swing a right, wondering why I had the idea at all if I wasn't even intending on considering it, and for the remainder of the trail I pass three people—a woman in her fifties in a coordinated blue track suit who's pumping her arms, synchronizing them with her legs, fists clenched, her eyes focused on the trail behind me, the rock music emitting from her ear buds muffled and loud, no reciprocated salutation, and two older ladies wearing capri pants and simple, ribbed t-shirts, hiking slowly and laughing, who, clutching each other's hands and watching where they step, scoot to the side, stop, wave and smile sincerely as if in total bliss on a regular Thursday, inducing me to imagine them not being afflicted by many regrets.

The park unfolds as I approach the edge of the woods, becoming vaster, the sky opening up when I ride out of the trail, ducking my head to avoid a low branch, and into the parking lot towards the entrance, where, daringly, I lean more than necessary into the curve at the end of a row of vehicles to coast through the stone entryway and under the pewter sign stretching between them that has the name of the park written in faded, saffron lettering. **KRAP SREBMAHC EILLIB**. My mom and I visited this park every weekend when I was a kid, but I never took the time to research who Billie Chambers is or was, and all my mom ever told me was that she was a kind person who only thought of others, and, gliding down the one-way street with cars, trucks, and SUVs parked to my right, past the empty baseball diamonds, then the soccer field where a team in navy uniforms are dribbling balls in a circle, I'm forced to brake without warning because a young guy with a bleached mullet yanks his green Toyota truck into a parking space in front of me, his music blaring, beating an elderly man in a station wagon to it. The senior driver honks his horn, screeching his tires slightly as he peels away, provoking the guy in the Toyota to stick an indifferent hand out the window to give him the finger while he continues typing whatever it is he was typing on his phone when he pulled in, all of which persuades me to veer onto the walkway once I've made certain nobody is nearby, my bike still squeaking, and I realize I haven't noticed the noise in quite some time. Despite the way the day began and the unpromising forecast, the park is much busier than I expected it to be, groups and pairs of people everywhere, most of the parking spaces, full, a line forming at the concession stand that's only operational in the summer, so, I hop off to better absorb the atmosphere, and, I'm not too far along on my walk when I pass a gathering of African families wearing matching red t-shirts with "Inalegwu Family Reunion" written on the front in white, surrounding the smoking barbeque grills. In a thick African accent, a bald father effortlessly executing balletic kick-up tricks with a multicolored inflatable volleyball encourages six youngsters seated at a picnic table to join him in the sand. "Come on, children. It's such a beautiful day," he says, motioning to them. "Let's play a game while the food cooks." All under ten, they're sharing a giant bag of cheese puffs, and with orange dust coating their fingers and beaming faces they spring out of their relaxed positions at the wooden picnic table, flinging their shoes off while scampering towards him. Laughing appreciatively, he puts his arms around them to calm them down, lowering himself and his voice to their level as he starts splitting them into teams, and his wife, who's wrapped in a bright neon patterned skirt, raises her spatula, waves it in his direction.

"Sam, we'll be eating in five minutes," she informs him, shaking her head, amused. Happy with what she's witnessing, she watches them lovingly before reattending the grill, flipping several burgers and pieces of chicken, then, accepting one of the two frosty drinks the relative preparing food alongside her is holding, she takes a sip from the straw in the cup. Beyond them, seven ladies are arranging plates, cups and utensils on the picnic tables, a jolly, plump grandmother placing a roll of paper towels at each end, wiggling her finger and telling her female kin this will be easier than chasing loose napkins across the ground, while the rest of the fathers and husbands chat and snack on chips and pretzels, and, in another fifty yards, at the edge of the park, where large, untrimmed hedges separate neighboring homes, also a section of the woods, septuagenarian women in pastel shirts and khaki capri pants roll bocce balls, their faces hidden under big, round hats with bows to protect their skin from the Sun. Close by them an Indian man in a lime collared shirt swings a golf club, his ball landing within feet of an entrance that leads to a recently cleared-out series of trails in the woods, taking a lofty bounce prior to disappearing in the overgrown bush. Throwing his hands up in disappointment, he doesn't bother hunting for it, and, dropping a new ball, he points the club at the teal water bottle he's aiming for, then, as soon as the four girls he's waiting on, who aren't paying attention, each of them engrossed in their phones, enter the trail, get out of his way, he practices three shadow strokes, swings again. The two basketball courts are full, games of five-on-five being played with a row of youthful boys, shirtless and sweaty in baggy shorts, waiting their turn on the sideline, yelling and egging on the competing teams while immature teen girls huddled in cliques behind them laugh and giggle, exchanging glances with them. All around people are lying on blankets lounging or eating, a few alone fiddling on their phones—a family of four shares a pizza, a short distance from them a stout, shirtless twenty-something guy in cargo pants snores, spread-eagle on his bunched-up towel, past him lovebirds in their thirties feed one another strawberries, each of them nibbling meagerly as they peer into the other's eyes, while an envious woman with braided black hair, in a floral-patterned summer dress, reading on a park bench, gazes longingly at them, her book in her lap, and, deciding this picturesque exemplar of a park won't get any better by walking further, I hunt for the perfect spot, when, out of nowhere, a tanned, middle-aged man on his phone who's wearing a toupee and a polo shirt with its collar popped, thick chest hairs and gold chains protruding from it, startles me by bumping my shoulder, aloof, in passing. His French bulldog sniffs the grass before setting its butt down, and, after slowly walking ten feet or so with no real purpose other than to see if my assumption is correct, I'm not surprised when I turn around to see he doesn't trouble himself with collecting his dog's poop, instead tugging impatiently at the leash, his tone irritable as he strolls off while rudely stating— not asking—"do you know who I am" to the person on the other end of the phone, which annoys me further, tempting me to whip my bike around to criticize him publicly, not about his pompous attitude, but his failure to observe easy, respectful etiquette—to clean up his dog's business—but I don't, it wouldn't make a difference, plus I have something else to do now, anyway.

I walk my cruiser onto the playground in the direction of the tennis courts, my feet sinking into the wood chips beneath me as I navigate my way through the safari-animal spring riders to spin the merry-go-round and sashay between the swings of a wooden and plastic jungle gym that's connected to a spirally slide with a gigantic green crocodile head perched at the top. Adjacent to that, two giggling girls climb the castle-shaped jungle gym, both in pink t-shirts with a Disney princess on them, just kids appreciating simple fun, and, like the rest of the park, the courts are full of players of various ages rallying yellow balls and enjoying what's unexpectedly become a sunny day. On the first court are four young girls, two of whom, both tall and slender, their shiny, auburn hair pulled back into ponytails, are identical twins; one bickers at her sister after she shanks a shot, showing her disapproval of the missed, easy, volley by teasingly swinging her racket at her face, the duo flinching when the sister reacts by waving hers in defense, and they continue flippantly lashing their rackets like they're in a sword fight while laughing, prompting their opponent, who is ready to serve to yell at them to quit goofing off. Figuring this is as suitable a place as any, I push the kickstand down, wiggle free of my backpack and reach in through the cluster of zip ties, ignoring the taser, searching, my fingers touching cold metal, eventually finding the rubbery black grip, and grasping it, I scan the park, my grip tightening the longer it sits in my palm, while images from earlier today reemerge and an itchy sense of dread creeps up on me for no reason other than that my surroundings seem a bit too peaceful at the moment as everyone around me carries on about their day completely unaware of what I've done or what I intend to do.

One of the twins screams when her sister collapses onto her knees, the racket leaving her hand and banging off the asphalt while she struggles to catch herself, unsuccessfully, tumbling into the net in front of her.

Laughing, but aggravated, she picks herself up, brushes her purple skirt, and jokingly scolds her double. "You should've gotten that ball, Analise!"

"Whatever, Amelia!" Analise snaps, laughing, mocking her twin by acting like she's tripping as I release the gun and fish out the crumpled brown paper bag that has my name written neatly on it in all caps.

Settling in the grass against a tree next to the courts, I remove my food and uncap and sip from the water bottle I stole earlier as I stretch my legs, cross them, recross them, and, while biting into my apple, numerous birds I can't see begin to sing, or maybe they've been singing this entire time and I'm only just noticing now. Over by the enormous rock covered in bronze plaques commemorating local residents who served and died in World War II, a tanned, muscular guy with a tattoo of the moon covering most of his back heaves a frisbee towards an attractive redhead wearing yellow shorts and a blood-red bathing suit top, who, catches it between her legs and slings it back to him, a golden retriever dashing back and forth in between them, jumping every so often, and the tattoo is remarkably intricate, with detailed craters etched into the surface of the moon and stars and a comet dotting the shadowy space encompassing it, prompting me to wonder if he mentioned the Sea of Tranquility to his tattoo artist. With all that's going on around me I assume the role I always do—the invisible outsider who melts into a crowd without having to participate—the tranquil pleasure of being near a gathering of people but not quite in it enveloping me as I chomp off several bites of my apple all at once while briefly watching a Hispanic couple who, fixated on their phones, are seated Indian-style on a blanket diagonally from me, him rocking, her perfectly still, then a balding man who jogs by them slowly, hunched over and breathing hard, his profuse sweating drenching his grey tank top, next a pair of squirrels scurrying up a tree on the playground, and, after unwrapping my sandwich and tearing open my bag of chips knowing that I won't eat either until I've finished my Granny Smith apple—I just like them prepared for when I'm ready—the previously happy lovers who were feeding each other strawberries quietly start arguing. Strawberry in hand, she puts her finger to her lips, hinting for him to lower his voice while checking their immediate vicinity to determine whether anyone's noticed them, so, displaying his anger in silence, he points at her phone, springs to his feet, and marches hastily to the top of the hill behind them where he walks in a circle, thinking. Visibly concerned and dropping her phone she pursues him, nearly cutting off a middle-aged husband and wife wearing matching, designer sweatsuits and gold watches, who, disgruntled and offended that they were interrupted in the tiniest bit, both mutter something negative while swiveling their heads, their obnoxious, curious gazes eavesdropping on the quarrel at the crest of the hill as they smile with amusement before strutting on arrogantly, and, particular individuals simply amaze me, how they act, what they choose to do. I just hope that whatever it is, they can work it out.

I prefer my apples cold, especially when they're tart, but I don't let it bother me that this one has lost its chill from the fridge at home as I take a bite while a gentle breeze blows through the park, my eyes shifting to a bunch of teens gathered on overlapped blankets roughly twenty feet away, imbibing liquor and beer, none of them worrying about secondary containers, music blasting from an orange speaker on a nearby checkered beach towel. Four of the girls, all dressed identically—jean shorts and bright halter tops—flaunt their bodies and purse their lips for photos, critique them, and, dissatisfied, rearrange themselves in different positions and stances to snap more while, a pale, tattooed red-haired boy wearing purple glasses and a bucket hat mocks them, striking funny poses as he passes a bottle of Coke to his friend, who, busy flirting, snatches it blindly and empties the soda into his cup. Annoyed by the sun in his eyes, he flips his hat around and continues hitting on the uninterested blonde fidgeting with the straps on her striped shirt while sipping at her drink, and when he offers her the Coke, she shakes her head, lightly smacks the hip of the girl beside her, who's dressed the same as every other female there, then, clutching her wrist, drags her into the conversation in an effort to hinder her ogling admirer, and after a few minutes of one-word answers to his questions, he gives up, tapping his pale buddy to join him for vodka shots, and, sighing with relief, the girl rolls her eyes before quietly giggling with her ally. There are thirteen of them, eight girls and five boys, all of them talking, none of them listening, their superficial and unfelt conversations growing louder and louder, each teen yearning, needing to be heard—contemporary society's conversation standard—and, searching the open cooler surrounded by scattered shoes and sandals that's stocked with cans and two liquor bottles, a handsome, shirtless boy with a defined torso plucks a beer from the ice and pops the tab, guzzling what must be at least half of it. Brushing his dark, shaggy mop out of his face, he shouts, "Hey! Who wants a beer!?" while shoving his hand in the cooler. There's no response as he loosely inspects the small crowd he's in the middle of and hesitates, with a dripping can at the ready, before finally throwing it to a stocky, bearded pal, who sticks his arm in the air and nods to him without speaking. A chubby girl in jean shorts adjusts her pink spaghetti-strap top, fixes her cropped hair, chugs what's left in her clear plastic cup, stands, and steps forward awkwardly, tapping the boy who threw the beer on the shoulder. "I'd like a beer, please!" she requests cheerfully, politely, extending the cup to him. "Nice day today, isn't it?"

"Huh?" He looks her up and down, squinting, assessing. "Oh yeah," he replies, waving at the buddy he threw the beer to, who is engaged with an attractive brunette and not paying attention to him in any way, inspiring him, when he hops off of his knees, to hurry over to the clique still modelling for pics, joining them at the last second for one. The girl's smile and effervescence vanish, replaced by an all-consuming look of shame and disappointment as she lowers her head and stares, dejected, into the empty cup for a subtle, heartbroken moment before shuffling timidly to join three girls who are talking nearby, who immediately let her know she's not welcome by turning their backs to her slightly, causing her to scan the group she's with, worried and uncomfortable, and I can't help but imagine her alone in her bedroom waiting for her phone to beep.

Finished with their photo shoot, the girls huddle anxiously, bobbing and shaking their heads until eventually nodding in agreement as to what pics they should use following a period of heated discussion. Having announced these plans to the party once finalized, the giddy squad requires an additional ten minutes to decide on a caption together, and, immediately after posting online, they single out the others with them, encouraging them to find their phones to comment, a few of the girls forcing them aggressively into the other's hands while monitoring to ensure it's being done. Social media has consistently resembled a running joke to me, people posting the best shot they get out of a hundred, smiling when they don't mean it, striving to keep up with their friends while begging for likes and acceptance centered around a transient satisfaction to compete for positions in a silly, feudal hierarchy that emulates high school. I've always felt frustrated with how easily I fit into a particular stereotype, the majority of society assuming I'm a certain way, treating me solely in accordance with my appearance, what I wear, the music I enjoy, or my hobbies, not by getting to know me—the main reason I've never had a social media account.

For the third time, a piece of bark is pushing uncomfortably against my back, so repositioning myself, I set my finished apple on the ground for a hungry animal or swarm of insects to enjoy later, take a large bite of my ham and cheese sandwich with mustard on toasted wheat bread, and cram a handful of sweet onion chips in my mouth while surveying the park, soaking it all up, appreciating the day and the weather the way everyone else here is, pretending I'm happy. But the tranquility only lasts a couple of minutes before my thoughts begin to wander, starting with the twins on the tennis courts, maybe fifteen, sixteen, their whole lives ahead of them, to the group partying across from me reveling in a summer free of consequences, the idea that youth is so, so ephemeral and the awareness of the evanescence of life and our fleeting existences overwhelming my brain; ignorant of this sad truth, the twins go on harassing each other between points, the energetic gang of minors carry on noisily, chugging beers and downing shots while continually changing the music without allowing a song to finish, and, still absorbed in their phones, unaware of how many months or years they have left together, the Hispanic couple maintain their silence, not making the most of the day, what's around them, or one another, the feuding lovers haven't returned, and oblivious to the fact that this incident will be reduced to a memory, the basketball court erupts when a nimble, black kid dunks the ball emphatically, inspiring the boys on the sidelines to rush out of their cool, casual stances meant to impress the crews of young girls watching nearby, to rub his head and pat his shoulders, as the aged women wearing oversized hats and pastels recuperate on benches, near the end of their timelines, their backs hunched while sipping on tea and chatting, and, the Indian man pumps his arms and club into the air after he strikes his target, pleased his practice has paid off, ignorant to the fact that he just as easily could become a horrible statistic as anyone else.

The relatives at the family reunion clasp each other's hands as they all bow their heads in unison to pray, Sam leading them with words I can't hear, when out of nowhere, the realization that every person here is living a life as vivid and complex as my own—that each one of them laughs and cries and feels and loves, has their own individual personality and thoughts and emotions and hopes and heartbreak, disappointments, regrets, and worry, a house or apartment with dishes and laundry to wash, closets full of clothes, TVs with movies on watchlists—hits me abruptly, for some reason creating the effect that every single man, woman and child in the park has suddenly started moving in slow motion. The players on the tennis court seem almost frozen, incapable of moving at a regular speed if they tried, like the dreams I have where I can't run faster no matter how hard I struggle; six of the girls mug for close-ups now, their hair suspended in the breeze that's blowing through as they kiss the air, while the boys shotgun beers after piercing cans with keys, foamy suds rising and falling slowly onto their chests and clothes, their shouting, distorted, weird and indistinguishable; a Siberian Husky scampers out of the entrance to the trail, a delay in his steps, his legs and paws hovering in the air as he's chased by his owner, who's reaching for the trailing leash, a panicked expression fixed upon his worried face; the open mouths of the family of four eating pizza are motionless, everyone holding a drooping slice so the father can snap a picture; the frisbee floats gently in the wind, creeping from the fingers of the lady in the bikini top, the dog that's sprinting towards her appearing sedated in the way his body and his blank stare, concentrated solely on the frisbee, switch directions; the Inalegwu's eat so slowly they'll never finish, their forks and spoons inching towards their lips; the elderly women mosey along at a sloth-like pace from the bocce courts to the bathrooms; the clouds creep… and, completely absorbed in the details around me, I raise my arm, open my mouth, and chew as everything goes on like this, engulfing me in a hypnotic trance similar to the one I experience when, from the comfort of my bed on a dreary day, I follow the raindrops that splatter and trickle down my bedroom window in a gratifying cadence...and, while I'm focused on nothing, everyone's actions practically halted, their pink lips speaking in slow motion and their speech resembling the parents' in a Peanuts cartoon, I spot an old woman in athletic shoes with an elevated heel laggardly responding to the blonde girl yanking on her wrist. Grinning widely, revealing her braces, the child whispers in the kneeling granny's ear while pointing up, at what I'm not sure, maybe a bird, the Sun, or the plane gliding by, but above is perfect, akin to the opening of The Simpsons, with cumulus clouds of various shapes and sizes inching from left to right in the light turquoise sky, so forgetting the tree, which wasn't comfortable to begin with, I lie in a supine position, my arms behind me and my head resting on my interlocked fingers, the nearly-finished sandwich on my lap. Knowing that I won't be able to relax until I do, I wipe away the crumbs on my shirt and attempt to discern any sort of shape or object in the white pillows, giving myself a number of minutes to configure an animal, a mountain, a person, a building or a car, but nothing materializes for me, the clouds simply keep on floating, and it really annoys me that I can't stretch out my arms, vault into the air right now and fly over and away from all of this to soar beyond the clouds I can't find anything in and breach the Earth's atmosphere while watching the vibrant red, green, purple, and yellow airglow most people think is blue that illuminates the edges of the Earth grow distant behind me, it and the Moon in a syzygy with the Sun, Andromeda, our galactic neighbor, my next stop. Another plane flies by, I pop the last bite of my sandwich into my mouth, abandon the implausibility of space, and imagine myself on the plane instead, leaving this city, travelling somewhere, anywhere, my forehead pressed against the plastic glass for most of the flight, relishing the ethereal sensation of looking down at the world through an airplane window and catching a glimpse of far-flung regions I'll never view in person, the excitement staying with me the entirety of my trip, but, my daydream doesn't last long when it's suddenly shattered by an abrasive uproar that grabs my attention, triggering the pace of life to revert to normal, just like that, before I turn to find two jackasses on motorcycles sporting leather vests with skull patches on the backs, no helmets, creeping by at a low speed while revving their engines needlessly, deafeningly, gaining everybody's attention in the otherwise quiet park. Shielding her ears and losing her smile, the young girl frowns, stops amusing herself with whatever she was admiring, the old lady shakes her head, the partying teens flip them off, the Hispanic couple start conversing for the first time, shouting to hear one another, and the customers in line at the concession stand glare, irked, as the bikers continue to rev their engines while pulling away without a care for anyone but themselves, and, briefly wondering what purpose it serves, how a full-grown adult can act in such a way, I choose to dismiss their idiocy and go straight back to my previous thought—peering through that airplane window—which, unfortunately, ends up soon reminding me of how little of the world I've seen or will see, what I'll now have no chance of experiencing. I deeply regret that I've never travelled to a US city or foreign country of significance, nor felt the anticipation of sitting for a passport photo knowing I had a trip planned; I rue the fact that I don't possess any photo albums to reminisce over, no memories to recall. It's not long before a new plane drifts by, reemphasizing all of this, so in an effort to distract myself, I return to my prior activity, observing everyone around me doing what they've been doing since I got here—enjoying themselves, me not a part of it. A trail of black ants has made its way to my apple, covering the browning flesh, crawling around and on top of each other, and with my subtle, persistent feeling of being out of place rising impetuously, I wonder how many of all the people here will do better than me—the customers waiting in line, the employees working in the windows, the twins on the tennis court, the two tossing the frisbee, the couple already back on their phones, each one of the Inalegwus, the ladies who were rolling bocce balls, the golfer, the four teens on their phones obstructing him, the man who was chasing his dog, the arguing lovers, the partying group, the family sharing the pizza, the napping twenty-something guy, the grandmother and granddaughter—who will dip into the reservoir of all the opportunities available to them? Who will visit the countries they still have the energy to explore? Who will develop the skills they still have time to develop, for the things they've always wanted to try, like learning an instrument, a new sport, or a second language? Who will chase after the career they still have the courage to pursue?

Peeking at my watch under my jacket sleeve I realize my break is up and, staunchly devoted to concluding my day regardless of how I'm feeling, I switch mindsets and jokingly scold myself for forgetting to bring a chocolate chip cookie or a bag of peanut M&Ms for dessert as I guzzle the rest of my water on the way to the blue recycling bin close by. I drop the bottle in, my trash in the green can beside it, neatly fold the crumpled paper bag at its old creases, slide it into the front pocket of my backpack, consider checking my phone but don't, walk my cruiser to the edge of the road exiting the park, my squeaks not attracting anyone's curiosity as I pedal off, and in the thirty minutes it took to eat my lunch, 3,442 people were born around the world and 3,712 died.

- noun : television programs, magazines, books, audience **oleka** - noun : the awareness of how especially in dim light **flow** - verb : (of a fluid more than a product of your circumstances **sequoia** - noun : a redwood tree, especially around you **pilot pen g2-07** - noun :

America's #1 selling Go-2 gel ink pen (NPD, 2021) G2 writes smoothly, has a comfortable rubber grip, and has been proven to write longer vs. the average of branded competitors

or criminal **euphonious** – adjective : (of sound, especially speech) pleasing to the ear **porn**

...ional aspects of a nonsexual subject and stimulating a compulsive interest in their audience

...de and outline of someone or something visible against a lighter background,

...tinuously in a current or stream **vaucasy** – noun : the fear that you're little

...end up looking back on years of labor with little to show for it **seq**

the fear that you're utterly powerless to change the world

or wicked (Activity) **sensuous or** the dark shape

nefarious – adjective : (typically of an action or etc., that are regarded as emphasizing the few days are memorable **silhouette** – noun : gas, or electricity) move along or out steadily and con **routwash** – noun : a moment of panic that you'll the California redwood **nemotia** – no :..

I LEAVE THE PARK, SWING a right, and in about half a mile I'm on Timberlake, a busy four-lane road I prefer not to bike on because there's no walkway and barely any room on the shoulder. Clearly exceeding the 45-mph limit, traffic whizzes by me, five drivers honking even though I'm not in their way and doing my best to stay as far to the side as possible—I'm not one of those cyclists who ride in the middle of the street, impeding the people trailing him and disrupting traffic, an obnoxious method that, as a fellow biker, I'm only able to view as either an act of pure ignorance or unwarranted self-entitlement. The bank that's repeatedly changed names since my grandfather retired from there decades ago comes up on my left, and after passing it, I yearn for a final view before it slips out of my sight, so I turn my head and a dented Honda honks at me when I momentarily veer over the white line, while a childhood memory of myself in a temporary sandbox enters my mind—*my mom and I are attending a party or event held by the bank in the parking lot and I'm allowed one minute to rummage through the sand for money, so I get on my hands and knees, wishing for a bill instead of a coin, digging and scooping, only to come up with thirty-six cents*—as I glide by a vacuum outlet, a nail and tanning salon, a McDonald's, before my thinking shifts from revisiting on this thought to assessing my day, what I'm compelled to finish, hoping I won't be caught before I do, and, feeling relieved because past the intersection of Waterlick and Timberlake, bordering the grocery store parking lot where the local high school students meet and gather on weekend nights, there's a sidewalk I can travel on in lieu of the street; I steer onto it. With the bus stop merely fifty yards ahead, I hop off, avoiding the cracks beneath my feet, when a shockingly loud exhaust startles me before a guy zooming by in a maroon truck with a lifted suspension, huge tires, his music blaring, flings a cup out of his window. Chocolate ice cream splatters the asphalt as he speeds away, swerving vehemently through the insignificant traffic to run a red light, the discarded polka-dotted container promptly crushed by a rickety, wobbly-wheeled station wagon, but the beat-up jalopy misses the plastic spoon, which gets lucky with a number of vehicles, dodging the cup's fate until a silver van splinters it into pieces.

An elderly woman in a brown sweater and corduroy pants clutches her purse in her lap on the bench, looking nervously for the bus, tapping her heels in unison and concentrating on the concrete between glances as loose newspapers rustle at her feet, while further from her a teenage girl with dyed orange hair, wearing a knitted stocking cap, a midriff black shirt, and ripped, black jeans, is perched on the backrest, her feet on the seat. Scrolling through her phone, she pinches her stomach and sighs, and a middle-aged man who's pacing back and forth and continually tugging at his green Subway shirt worriedly rechecks his watch, an advertisement for a resort in Jamaica, an island I doubt many in this area will ever vacation on, looming behind the three of them, depicting an ocean six shades of blue, pristine sand, and a line of palm trees, a bronzed couple in sunglasses, both toned, their teeth unbelievably white, relaxing under a striped umbrella and raising glasses filled with a frosty pink liquid as if they're about to toast, and, despite the fact that there's a trashcan no more than five feet away, garbage litters the ground—cups, cans, pieces of paper, napkins, hamburger wrappers, spoons and forks—various other bits of trash are spread all around the grass, at the old lady's feet, even a pair of soiled panties and a greasy beige t-shirt lie next to the hole that's been cut out of the hedges and fence. A shortcut I've used for years, it's a quicker route to where I'm headed that eliminates biking an additional mile down Timberlake, turning right on Wildwood, then basically backtracking up Wards. Yanking the chain-linked fence further apart, I maneuver my cruiser through it while minding my jacket and pants so they won't snag on the pointy metal, and, stepping over the wet, stained clothes, I'm dumbfounded by society's incapacity for self-government—how even when given the easiest, most convenient task, the correct, appropriate thing to do is casually brushed aside without the faintest care—which is why the notion of humanity banding together in the event of an apocalypse amuses me. People yell and scream when they don't get their way, react like children to the slightest of inconveniences, boil within if forced to wait in line too long at Starbucks, honk their horns madly with rage in traffic, judge and belittle people they don't know, strangers they don't trouble themselves with as far as understanding or becoming acquainted with them goes; they buy toilet paper and hand sanitizer by the bundles when there's a pandemic, disregarding everybody but themselves, a small percentage with the sole intention of collecting a profit by reselling needed goods online at exorbitant prices; they clear out supermarket shelves at the mere possibility of severe weather, ruthlessly greedy and uncaring of others, leaving no necessary products for anyone else. I could go on and on, but there's no reason to. Help each other? Please.

This section of the city is gray and dreary, nothing but repeating, harsh noises filling the air, a dirty film seeming to coat everything in my view—the street signs, the telephone poles with a variety of colored papers stapled to them, the walkways, the worn down, patchy asphalt I'm riding on, the near-empty, seedy restaurants, the pay-day loan stores with flashing neon signs, the auto repair garages and car dealerships, all the deserted, shoddy motels, the failed businesses missing windows and roofs, the pawn shops with items for sale on the sidewalk, the trash lining the road. At the end of the cracked, weed-filled parking lot of the vacant Kmart building that's for lease, above an enclosed drainage pond, a medium-sized billboard advertises a doomsday store that's running a sale, the gigantic, frightening black gas mask with neon-orange eyeholes in it looming off-center at an angle, randomly strewn, neon crosshair images circling it, with the words "Be prepared or be prepared to die" written in a menacing neon orange below, and at the intersection of Wards and Ridge I stop at the first of what will probably be numerous red lights. In an attempt to make it, a navy Kia revs its engine only to be forced to brake immediately for the rusted minivan in front of it that's in no rush and already decelerating for the yellow light, precipitating the mystery driver to slam on the horn as music blares from inside the tinted windows I can't see beyond, while not more than ten feet from me, indifferent by the noise, a haggard and disheveled homeless guy with a stringy, dirty beard grasps a sign that reads **HOMELESS VET PLEAS HELP, PLEH SAELP TEV SSELEMOH**, the letters scribbled as though a seven-year-old wrote it in the dark. Wearing a tattered, filthy green army jacket that has a faded patch I can't decipher on the right sleeve and a mesh hat with pins in it, he's teetering on the corner, barely able to stand straight after picking a cigarette off the pavement as a balding employee storms through the main doors of the furniture store behind him. Clad in his work uniform, a short-sleeved yellow shirt, khaki pants, and a wrinkled tie, he raises his hand once he's hurried between the disorganized cluster of dull sofas and recliners on sale under the shabby, fraying white tent. "I told you to leave!" he shouts, folding his arms. "If I catch you here again, I'll call the police!" He begins tapping his foot impatiently while the pasty, grungy vagrant gathers his twenty-ounce soda bottle and other belongings, a soiled rucksack and four grocery bags full of aluminum cans. He shuffles away with meager, shaky steps, his sign tucked under his arm, the light abruptly turns green, and, curious about how he came to be there, I pedal furiously, but I'm unable to keep up with the car heading to the next intersection, the music in the Kia dwindling as I tell myself I'll die if I can't while I wonder what decisions were made to land the vagrant where he is, then, I question if he's ever experienced a moment when he looked into the mirror one random morning years ago and his alarmingly different appearance made him aware of the dire need for a prompt improvement. Had it ever concerned him enough that he attempted to alter his former life choices for the better, but failed? Or had he simply shrugged it off, ignoring the shame and disappointment, and accepted who he had become and gone on with his days, leading to now?

As predicted, I have to stop five more times prior to reaching Kenwood Drive because none of the traffic signals run in unison, and, thanks to the constant whirring and banging noises emanating from the garage that occupies it, there's only one corner that doesn't have a homeless person waving a self-made sign or begging for money. With all four of the garage's bay doors raised, mechanics in identical, neutral uniforms are under vehicles or inspecting the insides of hoods, and, like this morning, like every day, it truly unnerves me that so few of my days have held any type of significance, that I've lived a life with nothing to show for it, but when the light switches I don't dwell on it, deciding there's no reason to review my joke of a story for the millionth time, especially now, so instead I focus on beating the next red, which I do. And to my astonishment, I beat the following two, then, while traveling through the next intersection, I realize I have experiences I have no idea I've forgotten, perhaps can't remember, and I try to recollect anything from my past I've suppressed, but all I'm capable of calling to mind are familiar memories that don't bring me any joy, so I choose not to exert the energy, forgetting about it once I reach the upcoming intersection.

While I'm waiting by a cell phone shop a tall, slender, air dancer gyrates a few feet away from me, it's neon purple body and silly, dread-locked head flopping all over the place the entire minute and twenty seconds I'm here, maddeningly mocking, as if it's performing just for me, ridiculing the melancholic trance I've been in all day, all week, and it takes the passing traffic for me to register the green light, that I can go, and, in my slightly flustered state, my foot slips when I push off and out of my momentary daze. One of the first structures erected after this city was founded, the decades-old brick train depot a block ahead that's being demolished, has essentially vanished in a mere two weeks, its remainders clinging to steel beams, rubble and debris scattering the ground near construction contractors and laborers in orange safety hats and vests gathered and eating lunch in a spot that's shaded from the Sun, and while pedaling by, the only man in pressed pants and a dress shirt who's writing on a clipboard points at the decayed, greying hotel across the street—with the peeling paint, three red-lit room window's, and the barred entrance, a vagrant comatose on the ramshackle stairs, an establishment that's notorious for prostitution and drug deals—eliciting laughter from the others as they nod in agreement and resume shoving tacos into their mouths. I refrain from pulling all the way up to the next light because I don't want the two women in skimpy neon dresses occupying the corner, their faces smeared with excessive amounts of blush and eyeliner, to approach me, and while I wait the blonde sticks her chest and butt out, motions to an idling SUV before strutting into the road, and, when the driver lowers the window she hikes her fluorescent dress to her hips to expose her lacy panties and leans in as her co-worker, who's too tanned and has enormous gold hoops dangling from her ears, pops a piece of gum in her mouth, chomps hard on it, twirls her hair, observes her partner, and suddenly turning to me, she scans me up and down, smiles, and winks.. Instantly uncomfortable, I'm not sure what else to do, so I stare at the black tar hoping the light will change soon. Thankfully it does, although not soon enough for me, the several seconds it demands feeling like they'll never arrive, but the Explorer stays where it is, the prostitute still halfway in the window aggressively putting forth her best effort to close a sale, provoking the man in the truck diagonal to me to forcefully honk his horn longer the second time when she doesn't respond to the first, polite, short beep. Startling her, she bangs her head on the window and jolts her torso out of the SUV. "Fuck you!" she screams, flipping him off and rubbing her scalp, before adjusting her dress, and, chuckling, he reciprocates by making a silly face while wiggling his tongue as she struggles to walk in her pumps back to her friend who's blowing a bright pink bubble.

Grateful that I've made it, I signal to steer onto Kenwood Drive at the corner with the jam-packed laundromat, dozens of customers, primarily of color, African-American or Hispanic or Asian, folding or prepping their laundry on tables inside, others on the slanted, uneven parking lot talking on their cell phones or smoking. Despite the crowded building, only a couple of older-model cars are in the parking lot, and by the dumpster a Hispanic guy with tattoos on his neck and cheeks sells drugs from a blue Nissan Altima with gold rims to a skinny, pale addict in his forties who's scratching himself and restlessly shuffling his feet, lingering eagerly until the dope peddler slaps a small package in his fingers and shoos him away. Cradling the tiny baggie as if it were the most precious thing in the world, his sublime happiness, the junkie grins before he surveys his surroundings while taking a few, slow steps that quickly become purposeful, swift strides towards the piles of old, broken washing and drying machines behind the building. Not far beyond that, fifty yards or so, Kenwood crosses over a trashy, green-filmed creek where a mangy black dog licks the water, registering me faintly as I coast by, and after cycling roughly a mile among the mounds of garbage littering the edge of the road, multiple rows of decrepit apartments, and a number of ramshackle residences, at least half with boarded-up windows or missing roofing, almost all of them blemished with various dismal, gross stains, the predominately bare yards full of discarded, obscure rubbish like appliances, furniture, even a toilet, I have to veer left to avoid a dead raccoon in the middle of the street. The trees are brown and withered, not much to look at, but regardless of this, I unintentionally start counting the giant, sporadic hedges I see lining both sides of the road, planted in thin, circular mulch beds as if they'd been intended as some sort of ornamental project years earlier to add character to the area, the majority of them now either dead or on the brink due to neglect, pollution, and last Fall's crusted leaves caught in the maze of bare branches unable to navigate their way free. One, two, three, four, five, six, seven—a striped cat sprints from under a van, stopping in the middle of the street. Frozen in a cautionary stance, it acknowledges me, glaring, before dashing off—eight, nine, ten, when out of the blue, "sequoia," comes to mind, not the tree, the word, how I've always been fond of the way it sounds when I say it—AIOUQES—eleven, twelve, the thirteenth hedge is in such bad shape, tired and broken, that I count it as twelve and a half, eventually losing interest, then, nine houses up, a brindle Boxer with a spiked collar trots parallel to the metal fence confining it to its patchy lawn, foam dripping from its lips as it chases me, snarling ferociously and jumping to no avail, its front paws banging against the intertwined metal when it collides with the corner, but still, I don't glance back in the dog's direction, I don't want to risk irritating it any more than this, the idea of this extra anger granting it the ability to hop the fence worrying me, and once his barks get weaker, farther apart, I slow down to a moderate pace, not because I'm tired, but because I need to conserve energy for what I'm about to do.

Bordering the muddy lot with the pair of oddly angled, double-wide trailers with bird's nests on their roofs, which seem abandoned and as if they don't fit in this dilapidated suburb, there's a two-story, beige home with darkened windows. A petite Asian woman, maybe twenty, slides out of the battered front door, barely opening it, "ASIAN MASSAGE" written unevenly across its front in cheap mailbox lettering. Dressed in a yellow robe that partially covers her purple lingerie, she sits on the stoop, crosses her legs, and lights a cigarette, takes a long drag. She spots me and gives me a scant nod with no emotion, checks her watch, and, seeing her here like this, perched on the stairs, terrible neighborhood, awful circumstances, lingerie-clad in the middle of the day, I unwillingly envision babies born into absolutely dreadful situations—poverty, famine, genocide, any type of horrible condition—and this triggers repressed memories of stories and reports I'd viewed on the news or online of emaciated kids with bloated bellies, bloody casualties of conflicts and drug wars, and bomb-demolished cities, tragic events that were happening on the other end of the world that we, as a society, couldn't imagine transpiring here, one of them a documentary I saw last month on prostitution, explaining how sex trafficking was rising in the US—California, Texas, Florida, New York, Ohio, the top five states—Washington D.C., Atlanta, Orlando, Miami, Las Vegas, the worst cities—the numbers were astounding, ugly, and a brief video of scantily dressed, underage girls bundled in fluffy fake fur coats wandering cold, city streets with cautious steps in high heels, snow falling all around them, was the visual that disturbed me the most. With no desire to continue watching exploited teens, I'd switched the channel, choosing to ignore it the same way I'd done with news recording atrocities transpiring in foreign countries, what a lot of people do when it isn't in their backyard, even though this was. She exhales a series of evaporating smoke rings, and wondering how this woman got here, I briefly conjure an awful, inescapable scenario involving a debt she owes to an illegal syndicate that can't be paid, a dire predicament that's forced her into prostitution—it's terrible, someone not having a choice or a chance at a life, especially a child born into a harsh, callous environment they have no control over, the fear that this is ultimately as good as its going to get growing every day while you're powerless to change the world around you, one that is such an awful, awful place. I've often wondered if there's a God, and if so, what God would allow such atrocities to occur. If he were all-knowing, he'd be aware of them, and if he were omnipotent, he'd be capable of intervening for the good, and if he were morally perfect, he would.

Not too far from my destination, in a block and a half, a shirtless bum whose skin is sunburnt and blistering comes stumbling towards me, yanking at his dingy pants that reveal he's not wearing underwear, and he spontaneously yells, "Uck you!", I think, through the uneven, grizzled goatee concealing his mouth, maybe at me, maybe not, so I drift to the left, not out of fear, but to avoid provoking by proximity. Holding up his pants at the waistband, he stops meandering down the road, chugs what's left of the clear liquid in the bottle he's clutching, then, finding it difficult to proceed, he slaps his palm on the flatbed truck beside him to balance himself before flinging the bottle. Not at me, onto the sidewalk, but, unfazed when the glass busts on the asphalt, he keeps staggering forward, what he's done doesn't trouble him, much like the choices that brought him here, I'm sure, the shattered glass remaining on the ground to cut a passerby's foot or puncture a tire.

The decrepit apartment complex I'm visiting, ahead and on my right, is similar to the rest of the buildings in this area, with a section of the rusted green shutters, damaged and split in the middle, hanging and swaying from side to side, a faded yard covered in trash, leaning air conditioner units propped up in windows with wood, and, scrambling frantically out of the entrance, a middle-aged tenant tucks his blue collared shirt into his khaki pants while jogging across the dying grass before pinning a nametag to his chest and jumping into an old, maroon Volvo station wagon that's missing a bumper, then, after three unsuccessful attempts, he gets it started. He revs the engine, a sooty smoke billowing from the exhaust, and I glide into his spot on the split, unlevel driveway when he peels off. It's almost comical how nothing of any importance ever worked out for me, just the occasional, insignificant victory that didn't truly matter in the long haul but gave me false hope, secondary triumphs that kept me exactly where I was. This community, that bum, the lady on the stoop, all remind me of myself in one way or another, as odd as it seems, and I wonder what percentage of local men and women share the same sentiment, felt like they had no shot regardless of what they did, but, having thought that, I'm also curious how many of them simply never tried.

Steering my bike by a black Ford Mustang without tires sitting on concrete blocks, I lock it for the first time today, wrapping the chain around a telephone pole, tugging to make sure it's fastened, then, turning my attention to the decaying complex with laundry drying on various balconies, I step between the numerous cracks on the pathway to the door that's ajar, the lock broken, asking myself whether I could do that, hang my clothes on lines for my neighbors to see. I probably could, but definitely not my tighty-whities, and, not caring if anyone sees me entering, I stroll inside and pass a row of mailboxes, a great deal of them unlatched and empty, to press the button in the foyer. The elevator dings straightaway, the doors sliding to the side to reveal it's graffitied interior—"I love Avery" is scrawled on the ceiling in red, a heart surrounding it, "IT AIN'T EASY BEING SKWEEZY," occupies the entire wall to my left in jumbo shadow letters, **YZEEWKS GNIEB YSAE TNIA TI**, "the thrill was here," is on the elevator keypad in white bubble letters outlined in neon yellow—and, not paying any mind to what else is written in the elevator, I push 4 and slip off my backpack while fixating on the numbers that are lighting up above the door as I blindly scribble the details of this appointment in my diary before removing my debit card from my wallet. I was given the option to have it personalized, with choices like a sailboat on the water, a mountain, the beach, clusters of clouds in the sky, or any image or concept I wanted to upload, so I sent the bank my best picture of Scrapdog. The elevator dings, the doors open, and, after I've scanned the sign in front of me displaying the apartment numbers with arrows below them directing which way they are, I go left.

Exhilarated yet nervous, a result of my unpleasant environment, I walk swiftly but not too swiftly through the dimly lit hall as several of the hidden bulbs in the moldy, vinyl ceiling flicker, a constant hum buzzing from them, the hand that's holding my card ready. Bits of trash and food crumbs litter the stained linoleum, there's a pool of chunky vomit reeking by a maintenance closet, and past that, at the end of the short corridor, I spot the one I'm searching for—#107—but before I can make it there a blonde girl who's no more than fifteen or sixteen years old with multiple scabs on her nose and cheeks eases out of the neighboring apartment. Tugging her oversized hoodie over her puffy eyes the moment she detects me, she huddles against the peeling wall, scooting by me hurriedly while staring at the floor, then a gaunt, tattooed, shirtless guy with bald patches on his head and sores dotting his skin as well, leans into the hall, yelling at her. "And don't take fucking forever like yesterday!" He notices me when he finishes his sentence, and pausing, he looks me up and down, then mutters, "You stupid bitch," as he slams the door shut.

Knowing that the lock to #107 isn't very secure, I wiggle my card between it and the frame, easily unlocking the door. The apartment is poorly lit, there's a coffee table with an ashtray and a pizza box on it, a tattered, plaid couch, a lone stool, at least a dozen porn magazines and DVDs scattered across the torn, linty carpet, and, after I quietly close the door, the oven light is the only help I have to see after that, so I let my vision adjust then slink into the shady hallway. There's a red glow shining from the bottom of a closed door, the muffled sounds of incoherent talking and moaning on the other side increasing as I produce the billy club from my bag, ignoring the darkened room to my right, when, the floor suddenly emits a creak on my last step, and, freezing in place, I wait, hoping nobody else heard it. The only thing that follows, I think, is a cash register ring seconds later, which seems odd, and, twisting the handle cautiously, I crack the door a few inches and slide into the room. Plain, miscellaneous tissues, towels, and clothes are strewn on the worn, cream-colored carpet, matching the living room's decor, and a cheap, triangular table with a lamp, red bulb, no shade, sits beside a desk against the opposite wall. Relaxed in a swivel chair and using one hand to type on a keyboard with his back to me, a scrawny older man in a soiled white tank top, with a green leprechaun tattooed on his wrinkled neck, pumps his right arm slowly then rapidly as I edge closer to him, the club raised. Wondering in passing what the tattoo means, why he got it, my shadow creeps along the wall, growing larger, looming towards him until it consumes his working shoulder, the leprechaun, his balding scalp, ultimately all of him, before his face reveals itself from the brightness of the screen, its stubbled, ugly, furrowed features becoming visible when he tilts his head to the ceiling while groaning in ecstasy, still unaware of my presence. I glimpse a small container of Vaseline, a bottle of whiskey, and an almost empty glass on the desk as I inch forward, the screen I can now see showing a naked Asian teen on a bed with pink satin sheets and an assortment of stuffed animals and heart-shaped pillows surrounding her, and, opening her eyes to grab a pink, tentacle-shaped dildo, she immediately catches me lurking behind him. Shocked, although there's no real reason to be, it's not about to deter what I plan on completing, I pause to see how the now visibly aggravated teen is going to respond. "Who the hell is that?" she complains. "If there's 'nother fella you must pay more."

The aged, liver-spotted man groans and frustratedly stops jerking off, then, banging the desk with his fist, he sits up and manages some sort of inquisitive grunt in response to her. Without saying another word, she points past him, shaking her finger, before wrapping herself in her bedsheets. Setting his palm on the greased metal armrest, he casually spins around to discover me, and utterly flabbergasted, he jumps back in his seat, then, regaining himself, asks, "What the fuck is this?!" in a slurred voice that suggests he's been drinking, so, I swing fast to prevent him acting any further and avoid any possible trouble, crashing the club against the side of his face, sending his black rimmed glasses into the dark corner to his left. Blood sprinkles the computer screen and two of his teeth shoot from his lips, falling and bouncing off the carpet while his body goes limp, his bare toes curling, compelling the girl on the screen to gasp and cover her mouth with her hands, dropping her sheets and exposing her flat chest as she begins shouting at me in a language I don't understand. Unfazed by the constant barrage of garble emitting from the screen, I start wheeling him to the doorway, and, he's not the least bit heavy, unlike the bulky guy this morning; he's so much tinier, weightless, really, but the rusty wheels on the chair don't move well, braking sporadically on the trashy fabric while she keeps yelling at me, slight delays between her exclamations as I wheel him out and down the corridor, her annoying voice diminishing, and, once I get to the bathroom, I can't hear her at all.

Akin to a public restroom I wouldn't use, his bathroom smells terrible, the obtrusive odor so bad that I pinch the tip of my nose prior to flicking the light on, and, when I do, the grotesque sight prompts me to lay my backpack in the hallway in lieu of on the stained tiled floor. With the faint, muffled noise of a TV emanating through the speckled, mildewy wall over the bathtub, I grab six zip ties and roll him near the edge, then, leaning him forward, situate his hands behind him, wincing as I take hold of the Vaseline-covered one. I fasten his wrists with four zip ties, the lingering odor of the nasty, unemptied litter box next to the dirty toilet hitting me hard by the time I'm finished, and, while inhaling through my mouth and exhaling through my nose, uncertain if it's helping, I lift him by the armpits, dropping him haphazardly inside the tub. There's a simple thud when he lands, followed by a short squeak as he slides into a vulnerable position that's perfect for securing his ankles, so I bind his feet together, then fish out the rusty hacksaw from amongst the rest of the items in my bag, accidentally snagging the interior, ripping it a little. After slipping on the second plastic suit, goggles and extended rubber gloves I bought from the elderly lady I lied to at the store, I suddenly remember that he doesn't have his glasses, and, not wanting him to miss a shred of what's about to transpire, I scour the bathroom despite knowing they aren't here before swiftly returning to the room we were in, where the Asian teen's been shrouded by a blurred screen, her or another performer's shadowy dancing flanked by "PURCHASE ADDITIONAL TOKENS" links displaying various options and dollar amounts. I find his glasses in the corner I knew they'd be in and snatch them up, noticing three credit cards on his desk along with dozens of erratic, disturbing drawings of breasts and vaginas covering the top of it, which makes my skin crawl even more than the bathroom did, then, returning, I shove them onto his nose, disheveling what thinning, greasy hair he has above his ears in the process, realizing for the first time that his lenses are cracked. Setting the saw by the tub, I backpedal to the vanity, place my hands on the cheap, warped plywood countertop, marginally registering the inconsistencies and gaps between it and the cracked sink, and lean forward, staring into the streaky mirror while thoughts of what I've done today emerge, flashes of screams mixed with blood and terrified, twisted faces, but predictably my facial expression doesn't change in the slightest as I blankly gaze at myself reflecting on these memories, and, unable to help it, I yawn, not a short one, but a lengthy, engaging yawn, not bothering to suppress the sound it emits even if it awakens the individual in the tub. It shouldn't be that surprising, I've slept terribly this past week, it just feels like an odd moment for it to happen considering everything that's going on, when all of a sudden, his cat appears out of the black hallway. A metallic grey color, it traipses slowly from the carpet to the tiled floor, quietly surveying the room with its yellow eyes as it makes its way towards me then circles me twice, brushing against my legs and, purring, snuggles up to me, so, figuring why not, I kneel and caress it, eventually nuzzling its nose, sweeping our faces back and forth, enjoying its fur and the funny sensation of its whiskers on my skin until the guy in the tub regains a portion of his senses and groans pitifully.

Removing my face from the cat's, I continue petting it as the man in the tub blinks, squints, then fully opens his eyes. "What? Wha– What the fuck!?" He begins thrashing in the tub, his skinny legs and small feet slipping on the porcelain while he fights to free his wrists, his ankles, a feat he has no chance of accomplishing, and, remaining quiet, I rub the cat's tummy as it nestles closer to me, glad he hasn't noticed us. I take delight in the unintended show for as long as it persists—his thrashing in the tub, yelling obscenities at nobody—until he stops abruptly, turns his head wildly to find me petting his cat, and, stunned, he maintains a bewildered expression for several seconds before he's able to muster a partial sentence, stuttering, "Wha—, wha—, wha—, what the fu—, fuck is this?!", no doubt even more fearful now that he's registered me and the strange, clear suit I'm donning over my clothes. "Who the fuck are you and why the fuck are you in my place!?" he demands, in a much more concerned tone, his distraught gaze shifting from my emotionless face to my right arm, then my left, eyeing my above-the-elbow gloves. All of this clamoring and commotion has startled the cat, causing it to jump and spin, land gracefully and scurry off, vanishing into the darkness, and I wonder if this is a routine it's grown accustomed to, its owner raising his voice, habitually terrifying the poor animal, and he carries on shouting a few, additional expletives at me, but I don't hear them—I'm too irritated he frightened the cat. Ceasing his hollering the instant I stand, his eyes dart frantically around the bathroom while he grapples to free himself, looking from me to his bound limbs between each futile attempt, and amused with all of this, I smirk, which prompts him to amp up his efforts by tightening his torso, shoulders, and arms to briskly yank his wrists four times in a bid to break the zip ties while he struggles and thrashes in the tub, shouting "Fuck you! Fuck you!" at me in between grunts. "When I get out of this tub, I'll kill you, you piece of shit!" It's impressive to witness a man feeding off of his own emotions, and, dumbfounded that's what he's going with, I scoff at him before grasping the handle of the hacksaw he hasn't seen yet. Widening even further once I produce the rusty tool, his eyes begin vibrating feverishly in their sockets when I start shaking it with that sneer still plastered across my face. "Holy shit! Why, why are you, what are you—"

And with no sound or emotion, robotic-like, I crouch, clutching his pathetic, slimy dick. "Jesus Christ! Jesus Christ!" He wriggles and wrestles as best he can, his eyes, wild, managing to push his twiggy, helpless self up the corner of the tub a few inches, every muscle in his body contracting, his legs flailing to grip the slick fiberglass, and, wondering how often he's visited the nefarious massage parlor I passed, I picture him staggering drunkenly through the littered street and knocking on the beat-up door, a nasty grin unfolding in anticipation of the service he's itching to receive, the girl I saw on the stoop earlier answering and immediately frowning before faking a smile and reluctantly letting him in. Tugging his penis, I start slicing it with a calm reserve I lacked in the prior killings, using unrushed cuts devoid of unabashed excitement, and, with sweat drenching his face and dotting his shoulders, he thrashes and wails like a trapped nocturnal animal, repeatedly banging his elbows against the sides of the tub, his bloated belly heaving spasmodically with each rapid, anxious breath while his effeminate shrieks grow in intensity and hysteria, allowing me to truly savor this with an even more sublime zeal, his screaming euphonious to my ears as his neighbor pounds on the cheap wall before raising the volume on the TV to drown out his squeals so they won't continue interrupting whatever program is on, and, after three slices, it severs completely. "Aaaaaaaaaah! Aaaaaaaaaah!" Rising an octave or two, he releases a cacophony of shrill howls with a ghastly resonance that I've only heard in the movies or cartoons as he realizes it's not going to get better for him—this is how he is going to die. Purple and vermilion threads and tendons dangle from his bushy pubic hair, which is drowned in a great deal of blood, the rosy, gooey liquid almost appearing fake the way it oozes and spurts out of his butchered crotch, as if the top popped open on a dropped bottle of ketchup, coating his legs, stomach, forearms, and pooling in the tub while he shudders, squirms, and convulses. I step back so that I won't get any more on me than I already have, but mainly to watch from a better vantage point because this is particularly pleasing to me given the reason why we're here, and I'm grateful I did when he vomits on himself twice and a rogue stream of blood splatters the wall to his right, then twenty seconds tick by, maybe thirty, I'm not certain, and, deciding I don't care what squirts on me, I impulsively stuff the vestigial appendage I've been tossing playfully in the air down his throat, shoving it in as deep as I can, forcing and holding his mouth shut with such a determined vigor that my arm shakes. He looks at me with scared, trembling eyes while floundering in his own fluids, his muffled sobs gradually fading in the little time it takes for him to die whimpering words I can't grasp because I'm smothering him, but they're short and sad, and when he sinks into the tub, no more life left in him, a single tear trickles down his wrinkled, stubbly cheek.

His sleazy, newly lubricated self is preventing the reddish brown liquid from draining, so quite a large puddle has formed, and, snapping my neck, I fling the bloody saw to the floor, cracking four of the tiny white tiles when it hits. Chucking the gloves in the same place, I unzip and shed the clear suit and pivot on my heel towards the mirror to discover red flecks spotting my face along with a minuscule amount in my hair. There's no chance I'm using any of the dirty, crumpled towels in the bent plastic hamper, so, tearing six squares of toilet paper from the thin roll on top of the tank, I turn on the moldy faucet, wipe my expressionless face, and in less than a minute I'm fit for the world outside. Grabbing my backpack, I barely register the grisly crimson figure slumped in the tub when he expels a sound that resembles air being squeezed from a balloon, which I show zero concern for or interest in before strolling into the dim hallway, past his bedroom, which I hadn't previously noticed, with its ripped, sheetless mattress and lone pillow on the floor, and, while the revolting apartment narrows as I close the door, I wonder who will now care for his sweet cat.

I've always loved the Pilot g2-07, the way it feels, is so smooth when you write. Happily scrawling this X with an added, emphatic flourish, I remind myself there's only two to go, then, while unchaining my bike, I hear indistinct arguing coming from the holey, screened-in front porch of the neighboring, run-down tan house with the tarp covering its roof. Clutching a liquor bottle, a man in his thirties wearing jean overalls storms out of the flimsy, wooden door, shouting and cursing as he makes it a point to slam it on the woman who's following him. She gives up on chasing him once she reaches the edge of the driveway, brushes her hair from her face, revealing a black eye, and sobbing and hugging a baby that's swaddled in a blanket, she calls to him, "Steve, please!" while he screeches off in his dented Tacoma full of painting supplies in the truck bed. She calls out to him once more even though he's rounded the corner, and, lowering her head, she trudges back up the rickety stairs, making me curious whether he's ever apologized, said he'll quit on a Tuesday, never do it again, promised he'd improve after swearing to her it'd be the last incident, and if so, how many times has she relented with a deteriorating, hopeful "yes," only for the problem to arise again and again with him inventing excuses at first, like he can't sleep or "it's the weekend."

Steering onto Dixon Avenue, I couldn't be more eager to leave this district, so with my sixth social call 4.20 miles away, I zone out for this half, refusing to acknowledge what's around me—the discarded appliances and trash and litter and garbage, the dilapidated homes, the comatose drug addicts stumbling along the sidewalk and across vacant parking lots, the honks and sirens, the prostitutes, the unhealthy stray dogs and cats, the demolished cars and trucks and SUVs stacked on top of each other in the wrecking yard, the smells, the vagrants talking and shaking their heads in disagreement with no one—because I don't want to anymore, fixating my attention on the hill ahead, pedaling rapidly to get there despite Dixon showing no sign of an end, as if it keeps going on and on into the horizon.

effervescent – adjective : vivacious and enthusiastic **saunter** – verb : walk in a slow, relaxed manner, without hurry or effort **liberosis** – noun : the desire to care less about things **akimbo** – adverb : with hands on the hips and elbows turned out **youth** – noun : the quality or state of being youthful; the early period of existence **murmurous** – adjective : filled with or characterized by murmurs **dulcet** – adjective (especially of sound) sweet and soothing (often used ironically) **quintessence** – noun : the most perfect or typical example of a quality or class **kudoclasm** – noun : a cascading crisis of self-doubt

THERE'S A BLUE AND YELLOW bricked inn at the upcoming intersection that's open 24 hours and famous for its Cheesy Western, a hamburger and omelet combination on a bun made popular by workers on lunch, truckers, and late-night partiers. It's just before Forest Memorial Bridge, a somewhat intimidating section, with its elevated walkway that sits at least eight or ten inches above the street, the bridge's railing feeling insufficient, awfully inadequate considering the height. Passing under the detailed, ornamental stone eagles a talented sculptor spent untold hours on seventy years ago that are perched high above on the lamp posts, I glance over and down to the bottom, two hundred feet below, scarcely catching a glimpse of the people strolling and jogging the paved trail, resembling slow-moving bugs, the row of road bikes overtaking them, a centipede, causing me to swerve slightly off my path, unnerving me so much that I focus solely on the small business in front of me, where a rotund Hispanic employee wearing bibs and a paper hat pinned to his dark, slick hair rolls a tub of ice into the "employees only" door of the modest cement building as I ride by. Oddly placed at the tail end of the bridge, it's a fish market I'd convinced myself was some shady, mob-operated joint when I discovered it as a kid or maybe a young teen, I have no clue why, but I don't try to recall the age I was or further contemplate the reason for this silly theory; instead, I start pedaling harder, eventually standing on them to prepare for the hill I'm about to climb, which is remarkably steep and lengthy. The YMCA uses it for the final leg of a well-known and televised ten-mile race that's held annually to raise money, the last mile looping around to conclude on the bridge, the old, Forest Library at the crest, the mark of the beginning of a welcoming downhill finish. Once I've conquered that, the incline mercifully evens out the closer I get to a little beige home, merely fifty yards up, with a red conical roof on the side patio, the arrow of the weathervane on top of it fortuitously pointing in the direction I'm travelling, and I'm dying to hop off, walk the rest of the way, I'm tired, my legs are burning, but the fire department is ahead on my right, and three firemen with identical, navy pants, t-shirts, and buzz cuts are on the khaki-colored driveway talking, their thick, tattooed arms folded, and they're all stout and intimidating, rugged, muscular. I can't quit now, so, dismissing my eagerness to, I maintain my momentum, my shoulders pumping and legs burning with determination as I ride towards the three of them—last October, I'd read an article in a men's magazine detailing how to maximize your workouts. It explained that you should incorporate additional, challenging exercises when you're nearly finished and already drained; this escalated exertion combined with fatigue is what would give you better results, increase stamina, burn extra calories and fat faster—I'd always meant to test that theory and add it to my morning routine, but I never did, now I never will, and the firemen carry on with their conversation while following me with their eyes, their three heads turning in unison, almost seeming to nod in approval at my relentless exertion, possibly encouraging me to strive for more, push it even further, but as soon as I'm far enough away, with nobody in sight to prove anything to, I don't get off, but I slow down considerably.

Approaching the mini-market I've not set foot in once,

I'm rarely on this side of town, two men, one black, the other white, both dressed alike in baggy gym shorts, shiny sneakers, and too-large t-shirts, are smoking by the entrance, and they're talking loudly and excessively, continually interrupting each other while moving their arms and hands with the enthusiasm of symphony conductors until a silver Toyota 4Runner pulling into the lot makes them pause mid-sentence and tap one another's waists in unison when a beautiful Black woman steps out of the SUV, the tassels on the gold stilettos at the end of her long legs complementing her dress and swaying with each self-assured stride, enticing me to imagine the clicking of her heels as they strike the pavement even though I can't hear it. With both men still ogling her, the guy in sunglasses lowers them after flicking his cigarette to the sidewalk. "Hey baby!" he shouts, popping out of his stance, straightening his clothes. "Fuck, you are sweet. Bring that ass over here." He taps his dark friend's chest for approval, gets it, and reverts to the way he was leaning against the wall. She ignores him, and he adjusts his glasses and calls out to her a second time, probably wrongfully suspecting it makes him appear that much cooler, as if he couldn't care less if she responds or not, and, predictably, she doesn't, paying them zero attention as she struts inside, this gross salutation hollered by a man loitering in a convenience mart parking lot far from the type of praise or advance she's seeking in life, which provokes what I'm guessing is his need to retain an ounce of dignity and prove that he's a real man who won't be slighted, so he retaliates angrily with "Whatever! Fuck you, bitch!" and "You fucking tease!" before the door shuts, and it's a shame that she'll be forced to deal with that again in a few minutes when all she wanted to do was go to the store.

It's odd to me how a neighborhood like the one I was just in, a section of the city in such despair riddled with crime and drugs and prostitution, failed businesses, ramshackle buildings, people who are unable to find their way out, can simply be separated from the rest of the city by a hill and a bridge, particularly from this area, with an expensive liberal arts college close by and the wealthiest community in this state, comprised of multi-million-dollar mansions, barely a mile beyond that. I coast by a street that leads to an amazing overlook of the Lawrence River, the homes dotting the banks, and the forest surrounding it, a view I've only come to see twice, both times when I was a child, an odd and sad fact given that it's not a great distance from my house—I could bike here in less than thirty minutes—but there are a lot of sights in town like this worth visiting, charming locations I should have appreciated more often and chose not to, fantastic, picturesque spots in my own backyard that I unconsciously, regrettably, didn't bother to explore. In half a mile, across the road, elderly dementia patients wearing sweaters and cardigans despite the warm weather are flopped on benches or shuffling incoherently around the fenced, grassy portion of Cavendish Assisted Living, as nurses with badges on lanyards dangling from their necks watch while chatting in a circle. Startled, a pair of orderlies jump when the double doors behind them crack open, forcing them to slide to the side and pull the handles to help. A girl, maybe seventeen, eighteen, is wheeled out of the shadows of the corridor, her neck and spine stabilized by a stiff vest fastened to the chair she's trapped in, her unkempt blonde hair tangled in the metal rods protruding from the halo brace above and attached to her skull, and, she forces a smile after the nurse pushing her bends down to whisper in her ear while stroking her shoulder. I couldn't even begin to conceive of that kind of life, what it would be like to wake up to that daily, so young, with everything ahead of you and nothing ahead of you, surrounded by dying lights floating aimlessly across this scant, confined plot, the cafeteria, the halls...I remember my grandfather in the three years leading to his death; there were stories of miniature green men on Coke bottles in his room at night, soft meals and a lot of Jell-O, awkward, drawn-out silences, my mom and I the only ones to converse while he stared at the ceiling and floor, his hanging mouth consistently leaking drool. "When can I go home?" he'd ask repeatedly. "I want to go home."

The rock walls that border and protect the grounds of Villenave College, **EGELLOC EVANELLIV**, stretch from the corners of the campus, extending two streets, and, since I'm feeling moderately guilty about what entered my thoughts minutes earlier—missing out on things that have always been right next door—I veer onto the sidewalk for a better glimpse of the campus. Various oaks, elaborate rose bushes, and perfectly trimmed hedges dot the huge, grassy lawn, which sinks in the middle, creating a pleasant, sloping crater—an odd combination for a business and certainly for a normal, residential property, but not here, with the colossal brick buildings, enormous white pillars, grand entryway, and prominent stairs complimenting it nicely. A female student with cropped black hair, wearing a plaid skirt and a grey blazer, with a square nametag taped to her chest, is guiding a group of parents and their kids on a campus tour; she stops the small crowd by the gated entrance when a father asks a question, as the majority of the prospective students seem bored, most of them either engrossed in their phones or scanning the sky, oblivious to the opportunity smack in front of them and its potential for impacting their future—if they so desire. It's a shame I never had this exposure, got to experience college life, but we weren't able to afford it, and I try not to imagine a twenty-year-old me relaxing in the indented part of the lawn that's perfect to lie on, completing nonexistent homework during lunch or cradling mythical books in my arms and laughing with fictional friends while we race up the main stairs so we're not late, or raising my hand in a made-up class and beaming when the fictitious professor says I'm correct, but I do, picturing all of it quite vividly, as if I'd lived it, until the college is out of view.

Still reveling in my phony, emotional high, I swerve left, signaling, onto Samuelson Road, where the estates sit far-off and unseen, their brick, stone, or paved driveways stretching over hills or through patches of trees, and, after cycling by a field with a red barn and five palomino horses grazing in a corner of the white fence, three gold and black locked iron gates, then a mailbox resembling the head of a green horned dragon, its post a scaly body with back spikes, I arrive at #52. Relieved that there's only one car in the driveway of the English country mansion when I reach the top of the incline, I lean my cruiser against the new blue Mercedes convertible with the tan leather interior and a pair of purple fuzzy balls hanging from the rearview mirror alongside a gold and maroon plastic parking permit for the local high school. With the driveway's tiny brown pebbles crunching under my feet, I stroll around the car, past the rows of perfectly manicured viburnum, onto the front porch, through the marble archways, and unlatch the ivy-covered gate that leads to the back, but before continuing I pause to scribble the info for this stop in my diary, and for no other reason than to verify whether or not I've received any messages relevant to my actions today, I glance at my phone and find no missed calls or texts, only a news bulletin I skim the first sentence of—a reality star has announced she's returned to Twitter after a hiatus, and, shaking my head that this is news, I do what I should have done all along: I put the phone in airplane mode, throw it in my bag, and decide not to check it again until I get home, if I make it that far.

Enclosed by a tall, wooden fence bordered by proportionate pink and ruby rose bushes cut evenly to camouflage its lower half, the backyard has a trampoline, a tennis court with basketball and hockey goals at opposite ends of its net, and, near the pool with the adjoining hot tub, a pretty, blonde teen girl in a pink bikini is stretched out on one of the cushioned chaise lounge chairs, her body bopping to the music she's listening to on her designer over-the-ear headphones. Unconcerned about being discovered and acting as if I'm supposed to be here, like I came for a swim, I select a staggered row of darker bricks making up the pathway that leads to the pool, to her, aligning my feet on the rectangular blocks, shadowing the complex, diagonal, zig-zagging pattern while sauntering in her direction, seeking any minute inconsistency in tint or design to prove something here has a flaw, and, ignorant of my own audacity, I put my hands in my jacket pockets absent-mindedly, coolly, *actually* kicking my feet up with zest on several of my steps, but I can't find a single defect, like everything else it's impeccable, so I gaze into the sublime sky, appreciating what's turned into a perfect day to be at the pool, and next at the firepit and wicker furniture with coordinated navy blue and green cushions under a gazebo adjacent to a barbeque grill, slowing to a glacial pace as I get closer to her. I'm not sure why. Maybe it's the odd sensation of feeling like I've suddenly transported into a catalog for rich people, or I'm subconsciously soliciting to extend what little time I have remaining, as if this unhurried behavior will somehow persuade me to believe it will prolong the day despite my being well aware that it won't, but it doesn't matter anyway, because before I know it, I'm standing behind her.

The neighbors on the other side of the nearby fence are exceedingly loud and boisterous, boys frolicking in a pool, splashing water and screaming until an adult shouts, "Hush!" telling them she's on the phone. Disregarding it, not even glimpsing in that direction, I silently slip my backpack off while bending at my knees with my torso straight so I can keep an eye on her, pausing when I set it on the ground and chance upon an inverted ladybug struggling in the grass, and, so that it doesn't get stomped on and squashed in the minutes to come, I gently brush the shelled-body onto my palm, toss it to my right, then rise slowly. Oily and glistening in the Sun, the quintessence of youth, bright and full of life, she sticks her hands in the air to inspect her pink nails, which match what she's wearing, as she bounces her head and dances in place to whatever she's listening to. While examining them from different angles she swings her newly painted toenails with cotton balls stuffed in between them from side to side in unison, then, snapping her fingers, she rhythmically, fluidly waves her arms in the air as her shiny gold bracelets slide from her wrists to her forearms and the diamond on her necklace sways between her breasts, but I don't sneak a peek down her bikini top or enjoy the benefit of a better angle, even though I could. There's an inflatable unicorn in the pool floating towards the deep end, a faint, precise ripple trailing it like the geese earlier, the Kelvin angle springs to mind, then out nowhere I envision a brown gazelle in Africa wandering lazily along the edge of a waterbed, sipping casually while, unbeknownst to it, a short distance away, a lion stalks among the dense thicket of bushes and trees.

Careful not to step on her phone or knock over the can of La Croix on the pool deck or bottle of nail polish next to it, I slink around the chair, pushing my sleeves to my elbows, positioning myself in front of her, and wait the few, anticipatory moments it takes for her to notice that I'm blocking her sunlight. But when she finally stops bobbing her head, swinging her feet, shaking her arms, and opens her eyes, her demeanor doesn't change—no rush of shock or awe manifests as I'd anticipated, just something else, something...normal. "Hey, baby! I'm glad you're here!" she exclaims in a sweet, excited voice, her eyes squinting. I don't respond as she shifts in her seat, awaiting a reply that isn't going to come. "Uhhhh, hello?" Another uncomfortable two or three seconds creep by, and, with her patience depleting, she sits up, lifting her right hand above her eyes so that she can see better. "Mason?" Now looking perplexed and showing a hint of a frown, her enthusiasm is replaced with dissatisfaction when she realizes I'm not Mason, then one of absolute disappointment and disgust the instant she recognizes who I am. Cocking her head to the side, and highly irritated, she asks, "What the fuck are you doing in my yard!?" in a tone that suggests I'm harassing her simply by being near her. She glares at me intensely before peering furiously around me at her house, then back at me. "Well, loser?! Answer me, you fuc–" Instead of lying in that chair, I've been picturing her yelling all this in her akimbo stance, and this mental image has only riled me up further, increasing my craving to hurt her, so I lunge at her neck, not allowing her to complete her sentence, struggling to straddle the chaise lounge at first, and it takes three blundering attempts after stepping through the rubber slats while clumsily grabbing at her throat until I'm able to balance myself and get a firm grip—*sensing danger, the startled gazelle whips its head out of the water to investigate and spots the yellow beast, so, frightened, it darts simultaneously in various directions with panicked, nimble movements, galloping aimlessly in a circle as the lion pounces.*

Immediately dropping her phone, the screen cracks when it hits the concrete as her slick, small-boned hands latch onto my wrists, clenching them intently, while she kicks underneath me, so I put my weight on her legs, leaning forward as she grapples to free herself, clumsily, repetitively releasing my wrists and clutching them. Gagging raggedly, she swings and jerks her head, eventually wriggling her headphones off her ears, and, inching down along her yellow hair, they smack the pool deck, tipping over the La Croix I'd tried not to spill. Donovan's "Atlantis" is blaringly playing from the headphones—she never had a chance of hearing me, which makes me chuckle, that this was the song she was listening to, it fits so perfectly with the pool and all, the water, and, seeing me smirk, she eyeballs me like I'm some sort of monster, and her frantic demeanor grows even more distressed when I reverse my expression, and with a look of determination, refocus my hostility on her. She mutters her first words, I'm guessing, "please, stop," but her usual dulcet voice is now gravelly and raspy, indecipherable, following that, the best she's capable of producing is murmurous dribble, all the while her face flushing increasing as her eyes begin to roll back into her head. She goes on and on, blabbering incoherent gibberish, the weak whispers between her wheezing, sniffled whimpers sounding sweet to me along with the repeating lyrics, when tears start leaking from her eyes, flowing down her cheeks as spit and drool form bubbles at the edges of her distended pink lips, and after roughly another minute she quits fighting altogether, gradually loosening her grip, her body slumping into the chair, and her eyes slowly shut.

Uncertain if she's dead yet and still hovering over her, I don't give her any consideration whatsoever while assessing what's around me—the pool and hot tub, the tennis court, the trampoline, the fire pit—wondering what it'd be like to have these possessions at your disposal every day, things you'd never known what it was like to be deprived of. I've always had a desire to care less about things, to live my life without so much worry, and it's safe to speculate this standard of comfort would be extremely helpful. Briefly visualizing myself swimming laps, I prolong my fantasy by adding a fruit assortment to the round wooden table across the water, and now I'm munching on raspberries, strawberries, and blueberries while I lounge in one of the striped chairs, no hassles for the day, when my mirage is suddenly interrupted by her neighbor. "Quiet the fuck down, I'm finally off hold!" the mother curses, closer than the last time I heard her. I can't fully decipher what she's saying when she's not shouting at her kids, maybe placing an order, but, believing that the woman on the phone won't be drawn out of her yard regardless of the amount of noise we make, I scoop up the toppled can of La Croix, which is surprisingly still half-full, and covering the hole with my thumb, I shake it while the phone segues from "Atlantis" to Earth, Wind & Fire's "September," then, jamming the can under her nose, I shoot green foam and soda up her nostrils, inducing both of her eyes to open at once while she gasps for air like she was abruptly awoken from a dream she wasn't enjoying. Coughing violently, greenish snot shoots out of her nose, mixing with the mascara and makeup running down her cheeks, and her arms and legs jolt spastically as if her perception was lagging behind her body. Unable to mark the passage of time—a state I've been familiar with this past week—it takes a moment for her to realize where she is, what's going on, and, wanting her to remain lost, I seize her throat and throw everything I have in me, every ounce, into crushing her jugular, larynx, trachea and carotid artery, as if my life depended on it, like I'd die if this didn't happen. Requiring more energy than I expected, I maintain the pressure, my arms beginning to tremble the longer this continues, when I notice a miniscule daub on her forehead concealing a pimple, which, causes me to hesitate for a nanosecond and relax my firm hold before immediately returning to what I was doing, choking the life out of her while she tussles to free herself from my grasp, clawing at my arms, chest, and face, her legs kicking and flailing—*swiping its paw at the gazelle, slicing its nose and its right eye, the lion pounces on top of it, sinking its teeth into the helpless animal's furred stomach.*

One of the boys next door screams and, crying, calls for his parents, provoking his mother to raise her voice, but not to check on her child, nor to inquire about the commotion coming from here. "What do you mean you ran out of pepperoni?!"

Guttural noises splutter from the mouth of the teen under me as she makes vigorous attempts to breathe, her skin tone turning a bright rose with a hint of purple and blue mixing in, while she grabs at my jacket, then my shirt, tugging at it frantically, untucking it and ripping a hole near the hem.

"You're a pizza restaurant, how is that possible?!" There's a pause, then in a harsher tone and what must be her go-to response when her heightened and unjustified sense of prerogative is threatened, she snarls, "I want to speak to the manager!"

With a last-ditch, pathetic effort, the teen under me lets go of my left wrist, extending her arm towards the fence, her spread fingers a beautiful pink in the Sun, pleading for the miserable, unreasonable female voice to rescue her. I highly doubt she knows her neighbors well, most don't, hundreds of people living around you that you rarely meet, if ever, much less become acquainted with, and I can't help but speculate as to what's transpiring in her mind these final seconds of her life—if she's recalling her family and happy memories, like Christmas, Thanksgiving, birthdays, eating dinners together in the dining room, when she received her new car, parties at this pool—happy and sweet thoughts that rapidly and disturbingly shift to how she won't graduate high school or attend college, get married, or see tomorrow—all of these images flashing by only to end with the worst possible conclusion—that she has no future—*motionless save for its body's sporadic jolting, the gazelle gasps its last breaths of air on the edge of the bank, its eyes quivering in horror as it's devoured alive, the lion ripping muscle and tissue with its teeth and claws while surveying the river and grassland around him, unbothered by the flies swarming the air in anticipation of laying their eggs in the soon-to-be rotting flesh.* The veins bursting in her teary eyes are filling them with blood, and she looks so lost, before they roll back into her head again as her squealing continues getting quieter, until she can't even whisper anymore, the tingling sensation in my hamstrings continuing to build and reaching a climax when she releases her already soft grip once I hear her bones snap and then they, along with her arms, drop limply to her sides as her eyelids calmly lower for good, her effervescent existence extinguished.

Swinging my leg over the chair, I crack my neck, adjust my glasses and pants, tuck my ripped shirt back in, and scan her body, from her cotton-stuffed toes to her wild, disheveled hair. Laid out like a discarded rag doll, her four limbs hang off of the chaise lounge in such a way they create the impression they're full of sand, then, as if by design, her eyes suddenly open wide and her head rotates mechanically, inch by inch, stopping to stare at me expressionlessly, her mouth agape. Slightly flinching, I close my eyes, shake my head, count to five, and hesitantly raise my right eyelid to take a peek, finding hers eyes closed, as they should be, and, breathing a sigh of relief, I reassure myself she's dead, gone, never coming back. Remembering that she tore my new shirt, I poke my thumb through the substantial hole, irritated at first, but my minor, negative reaction vanishes and is replaced with a gratifying content when I picture her on a cold, metal slab in the morgue with a sheet shrouding her corpse from the neck down, a syringe, ladle, pliers, scissors, scalpel, chisel, saw, and forceps on the table next to her, and an obese, grey-bearded coroner in a stained white lab coat eating a sandwich while writing whatever it is coroners record about an autopsy as the female cop working the case, who's visibly irked by his apathy, sighs and exclaims, "Marco!"

Several silent seconds tick by. "*Polo!*"

"*You have to say it faster than that!*" The damaged phone on the pool deck beeps then begins ringing, interrupting the last few lyrics of "September." The caller ID reads *Mason*.

"*Marco!*"

"*Polo!*" Much quicker this time.

"Be quiet! I'm trying to order!" the lady next door demands, banging something made of glass.

Skipping through the covered gate and onto the porch, I clear the three stairs in a single leap, slide my fingers from the hood of the Mercedes coupe to its windshield, along the roof, down the tail, enjoying the crunching sound and the soft feel of the pebbles under my feet, and, reminiscent of a character naturally strolling away from an explosion in a movie, I leisurely walk my bike to the top of the hill without bothering to glimpse back at the immaculate mansion, happily marking this entry in my diary once I'm there.

As I reach the edge of the driveway and hop on my bike, a mailman parks his truck, lifts his sun hat, and checks both ways prior to crossing the street to stuff an armload of various-sized envelopes in an ornate, black and gold mailbox, when, I hear faint music, but I can't tell where it's coming from. A bright orange corvette screeches around the corner from the direction I came from earlier, the volume of the music increasing, the engine revving, windows down... Mason. I know I've been spotted at the end of a driveway I have no business being on, so, distressed, I immediately push off, hoping that it won't matter or that I got lucky, that he didn't see me, or maybe he did, but doesn't care, but he leans out his window as he approaches, staring curiously at me while braking, making me regret my decision to behave so lackadaisically two minutes ago. Slowly meandering past the mail truck because I've forgotten to use my legs, I try to act nonchalant by casually glancing at the mailman opening a box, at a clump of trees, another driveway, its gate locked, the nearby woods, but, unable to stop myself, I whip my head around to look again. Already in the driveway, Mason springs out of his car, puts his hands on the roof, watches me with a perplexed expression, and now, quite the opposite of an indifferent character in a film, I start pedaling frantically as a cascading crisis of self-doubt engulfs me, and, with my mouth suddenly dry and my palms sweaty, in an attempt to convince myself that this can't befall me—there's no way it could end like this, I have to get to the most important part of the day—as well as to make the next 3.7 miles feel shorter, I choose to only think of things that bring me joy:

defenestration – noun : the action of throwing someone out of a window

heartspur – noun : an unexpected surge of emotion in response to

incendiary – adjective (of a device or attack) designed to cause fires

ineffable – adjective : too great or extreme to be expressed or described in words

wafting – verb : pass or cause to pass easily or gently through or as if through air

swish fulfillment – noun : the feeling of delicate luck after casually tossing something across the room and hitting your target so crisply and perfectly that you feel no desire to even attempt another shot

epoch – noun : a period of time in history or a person's life, typically one marked by notable events or particular characteristics

elixir – noun : a magical or medicinal potion

THE SMELL THAT FOLLOWS RAIN, a Coke from the freezer with frozen M&M's, the wash and massage prior to my haircut, the brushes on the sides of escalators, beating a game on beast mode on my PS4, the Sun on my skin, my voice after inhaling helium, being up before dawn and hearing the tranquility of a world that hasn't awoken yet, discovering a good series on Netflix, Amazon, or Hulu with several seasons and lots of episodes, a friend or acquaintance using my name in conversation, waking up before the alarm and realizing there's more time to sleep, staying in bed while it snows, tacos, seeing bus drivers wave at each other, replaying a video game I loved when I was younger, the scent of fresh-cut grass, Hans Zimmer, remembering a pleasant dream, organizing my comic book collection, smooth, downhill slopes on a bike ride, people smiling at me for no apparent reason, sunlight shining through my bedroom blinds, the wind hitting my face, extra fries at the bottom of my takeout bag, new Marvel movies, reading Donald Ray Pollock books in my backyard swing, stumbling upon a coin that's from the 1950s or earlier in my change, meaningful conversations, awakening to a Sunday with nothing to do, smiling at a child I see in public, laughing so hard it hurts, the sound of ice in a cup crackling when I pour water into it, watching the sunrise, warm clothes out of the dryer against my skin, being the first person to stick a knife in a jar of peanut butter, the sound of the wind blowing through the trees, waking up and realizing it's a gorgeous day, raindrops tapping on my window at night, ice cream, laughing at a joke or scene from a movie or comic book I remembered spur of the moment, seeing the lines and patterns in my carpet after vacuuming backwards, a stranger holding the door open for me, walking barefoot in grass, the goosebumps a certain song gives me no matter how many times I hear it, popping bubble wrap, getting a perfectly folded kettle chip in my bag of chips, the feeling of a fresh haircut, the first, long stretch of the morning while still in bed, seeing a fresh coat of untouched snow, finding a perfectly shaped pebble I'm compelled to bring home, observing the sunset, having a public restroom all to myself, a pencil with an eraser that doesn't smudge my paper when I use it, recognizing the unforeseen beauty of nature and stopping to appreciate it, the first several bites of cereal that are crunchy, but also contain milk, a sunny day, anything organized by color, eating breakfast in bed and watching TV, being asked by someone who cares about me how I'm doing, the cool side of the pillow, rainbows, finding out how many peas can fit on the teeth of my fork, *True Romance*, making small talk with a stranger, the tiny squeaking sound I get when I rub two pickles together...

Decelerating for the blinking red warning signal that hangs above the intersection ahead of me and directs me into a new neighborhood, I glance left, right, another, quick left, a milk delivery truck the only vehicle I see coming this way, but it doesn't matter, it's fifty yards away, so I keep on, and the vehicles and all the houses look the same, blurring as I race by, focused on what's ahead of me, my cruiser squeaking, and now gripping my handlebars tighter, I worriedly concoct a scene in which there are police cars waiting for me around the corner, four of them blocking the road, their sirens blaring, red and blue lights flashing, officers positioned behind them with their weapons drawn, instructed to shoot on sight.

...the smell of books, hopping back into my nice, toasty bed after needing to get up for something in the middle of the night during winter, guessing the next line in a movie even though I haven't seen it, standing in front of the air conditioner on a hot day and positioning myself so it blows right up my shirt, hearing the birds chirping in the morning for the first time in months when spring arrives, achieving a modest victory like washing the dishes or finishing the laundry, being in that semi-sleepy state where every time I switch positions in bed it's more comfortable than the last, pulling a Coke out of the freezer just before it's started to freeze, watching my breath float away in cold air, the ambiance and aroma of the old skating rink, receiving extra nuggets in an order at Chick-fil-A, peeling off the protective film from screens, the sense of relief after being startled and realizing I'm safe, looking up in the middle of a thunderstorm to witness the sky explode, Q-tips in my ears following a shower, sitting on a hallway floor wearing untangled headphones with my back against the wall and toes touching the other one, the crackling sound of burning wood, linking my toes together when I'm lying in bed, seeing the pile of paper and ribbon left on the floor once all the Christmas presents have been unwrapped, watching a person I care about open a present I gave them, the Fall air, eating the airy puffballs that sporadically appear on pizza, giving out Halloween candy, going down the up escalator, chocolate, freshly baked bread, taking that first sip of soda that tickles my nose and suddenly being able to breathe again, *Cloud Atlas*, the lingering scent of perfume in an empty elevator, removing my shoes after a long day, wearing rain boots and strolling through deep water, the fragrance of milk-and-honey body shampoo, slipping on brand new socks, watching a flock of birds change direction in the air, learning something new, stopping the microwave just as the beep is about to say it's done, plugging my USB in on the first try, finding money that I didn't know I had in my pocket, running into people walking their dogs, clean counters and no dishes, the scent of gas, a handwritten letter, the sensation of warm sand between my toes, the smell of comic books, hot tea, seeing the Sun shine through the clouds in such a way that I believe there has to be a heaven, traveling under a tree and being surprised by the shadows all around me, déjà vu, summer nights, listening to a flowing river, an outdoor lunch, hearing a dog bark quietly while it's dreaming, cows, random acts of kindness for someone else, a brand new Pilot g2-07, red, the smell of the ocean, tracking my packages online, sleeping in freshly, washed sheets, gazing into the night sky when it's full of stars, a whiff of sunblock, listening to sad songs that provide an emotional release, seeing the underdog win, dancing like nobody is watching...

Despite my efforts to concentrate solely on pleasant thoughts, dread and defeat persist on creeping up on me as I ride by a law office, a bank, a cupcake shop attached to an Italian restaurant, and two other banks, so I handle it the way I've handled negative situations like this all my life and wait, longing for it to cease, the pressure building in my shoulders, my chest, and the rest of my body while I suppress any presumptive ideas about the law and failing, but, biking feels difficult, my Jell-O like legs uncoordinated, and the short distance that remains feels endless, like I'll never get there, but before I know it I'm on Horizon

Drive, and after speeding by the house with the colorful garden gnomes, I'm astonished to find myself off my bike, the kickstand already down, standing outside of my final destination.

"Hi! Hi!" I hear, in an exuberant, sweet voice, drawing me out of the fog I was in. I spin around to see the frail elderly lady who lives across the street approaching me enthusiastically, the extra skin on her veiny arms jiggling as she waves, mail tucked under the other arm, and I reciprocate her greeting but motion for her to stop. Putting one finger to my lips, I point at the ranch home I'm preparing to enter, which amuses her, so she nods that she understands, doesn't want to ruin the surprise, and, giving me two thumbs up and a broad grin, she begins examining her mail, shuffling through it eagerly before ripping open an envelope dotted with multiple dollar signs encircling the brightly lettered words *YOU MAY HAVE ALREADY WON!* accompanied by an arrow pointing to her address, then, straining to read it, she inches back down her driveway. Turning back to face the ranch house, I take a brief moment to remind myself that I've made it, I'm *actually* here, before striding past the dented mailbox, only marginally registering it and the tall grass that needs to be cut, the rusted, oil-leaking Chevy truck parked under the slanted, rimless basketball goal, the slow drip forming a small puddle on the worn gravel driveway beneath it, the shingles missing from the roof, the empty pots and split bags leaking soil into the thin mulch bed, the weedy cracks I half-consciously avoid on the walkway, and, hopping up the crooked, deteriorating stairs to the peeling blue door, I stand on my toes to peek inside the dirt-obscured window, eventually catching sight of an old man asleep in a recliner in the middle of the living room.

I push cautiously on the unlocked door, the knob clicking softly as I twist it, to ensure there's no abrupt creak that may startle him, while pausing to check if the neighbor's snooping, but, now on her front stoop, she's still struggling to read the letter in her fingers, so I lock the door quietly behind me and sneak to the top of the four steps. The stale air reeks of alcohol and cigarettes, the strong stenches collectively wafting together even more potently when I reach the living room, the kind of odor I'm confident I'll smell on my clothes afterward as the ceiling fan spins at a barely-there pace, doing little to help as it emits its constant hum, dust coating it and everything else—the TV in the corner showing a baseball game, the three buck heads mounted to wooden plaques hanging on the wall above him, the stuffed fox and raccoon staring at me from opposite ends of the fireplace, the dining room table and gun cabinet behind it, its glassed doors open with various hunting rifles bunched together and leaning haphazardly, which tempts me to simply pick a random gun, stuff it into his mouth, and squeeze the trigger, but, as suddenly as this idea comes to mind, I dismiss it as rash and too humane.

He's wearing one sock, striped boxer shorts, and a black t-shirt with a silhouette of a fisherman carrying a rod and tacklebox that reads *I'm on a mission, I'm goin' fishin'*, and he's either blacked out or sleeping, I'm guessing the former, on a tattered, yellow, floral-patterned Lay-Z-Boy with wooden handles, his head tilted and facing an antique mahogany table butler to his right. On it there's a pack of cigarettes, a sleep apnea machine, a lighter, and a half-filled glass of brown liquid next to an overflowing ashtray, a thin strand of smoke rising from an unfinished cigarette propped on the pile of ash, and, with one hand tucked inside his boxer shorts, his belly rising and falling, he continues snoring steadily like I'm not here. Given the smoke, I figure he hasn't been out long, but his heavy snoring eases my worry of him awakening for now, so I take my time to survey the room—a plaid sofa covered in magazines and towels, a record player and wooden box of classic records beside it, empty beer bottles and a mug on the coffee table—stopping when I notice the ray of sunlight shining through the gap in the unevenly closed shades that's now brightening up this lone slice of the living room, dust motes suspended in its beam, and, deciding it's time to finish what I started, I turn to the kitchen.

Soiled towels and various greasy tools lie in a pile on the edge of the counter, dirty dishes cram the sink, two of the doorless cabinets are filled with cups and bowls and plates stacked on top of each other in disorganized piles, and boxed medicines and numerous bottles, most containing pills, the rest green and dark liquids, crowd the shelves of another cabinet, its wooden door hanging by a broken hinge above the stove, which is stained with solidified blotches from previously cooked meals, and, spotting just what I came looking for, the whiskey bottles huddled in a group near the fridge, I eagerly grab a few of their necks without thinking, clinking the glass together. He breaks his cadence with a boisterous snort followed by gurgled wheezing and then coughs loudly, causing me to immediately release the bottles and freeze mid-step out of habit. Holding my breath and focusing on the smudged linoleum floor, I try not to make any more noise, the next several seconds seeming like an eternity until he reverts to inhaling and exhaling hard, sustaining this harsh, rhythmic racket in a manner that convinces me he's not waking up, but to be certain I creep towards the recliner, tentatively resting my palms on its back, to confirm. This is the closest I've stood to him since I've been here, and he smells terrible. His salt-and-pepper hair is greasy, his fingers and nails are blackened with oil, and I can now confirm that he's not asleep but blacked out, because along with cigarettes, his mouth smells like a bar. I've always wondered how often an alcoholic has assessed his or her life, known the decisions being made were a waste, not the ones they should be making, yet kept on, drinking before noon and into the night, enduring rough, hungover mornings, sparking unwarranted arguments with spouses, screaming at children, justifying that it's worth it, failing to consider tomorrow, unaware of how it's affecting them and those around them, or worse, knowing and not caring, refusing to do better for themselves through will and determination or to seek help from programs or sponsors.

Realizing there's no need to be pushing my luck and risking his coming to and overpowering me to get to one of the guns, I drop my backpack on the couch to grab the weapon I'll be using for the last time today, and, wanting this to be as personal as it can be, I position my face inches from his as I raise the taser. His breath is disgusting, like he hasn't brushed his teeth in days, as is the white sauce smeared among the sparse hairs dotting his chin from his poor shaving job, forcing me to gag, and, increasing the electric charge to full power I jab him directly there, in the fold under his mouth, inducing his eyes to open in a flash as his head jerks wildly and his shuddering torso jolts into the air before falling back into the recliner. After regaining a meager portion of his senses, he whips his head in my direction, his confused expression morphing into one of anger as he grunts and tries to jump out of the La-Z-Boy, his extended arms and fat fingers reaching for me, but I don't let him get far, tasing him in the left cheek, driving him right back to where he was, then, for some reason, I begin attacking him like I'm a fencer, bending my knees, lowering my stance, and throwing my other hand in the air while I jab at his stomach and legs and chest with dashing strokes from the left, ending on his neck. He reminds me vaguely of popcorn as he flops around in the chair, which amuses me for longer than it should thanks to my out-of-the-blue elation, and once I'm satisfied that he's been neutralized after I've held the taser against his wrinkled skin for an extra, unnecessary, slow count to five, with my other hand on my hip, I retract the taser as if it were a sabre and gradually lower it.

The volume on the TV raises noticeably when a commercial comes on between innings—this has always annoyed me—the high-angle camera scanning a cluster of elderly people slowly and cautiously hiking a trail in the woods, and a women in a peach sweatshirt with kittens on it complains that she has to go the bathroom, three others agreeing that they do, as well, before the camera pans past them, zooming in on an attractive guy at the rear of the group who stops and crosses his arms while they push on. Similar in age to the man I've come to visit, he's wearing a purple sweater and pleated, khaki pants, has silver hair, a silver moustache, and with a compassionate, empathetic tone, like he genuinely cares or he's experienced it, he asks, "Do you often feel the urge to urinate?" Pausing and interlocking his fingers at his stomach, he adds, "Do you wake up frequently at night?" and "Do you dread extended periods of time in public?", his deep, pleasant voice resonating across the otherwise mostly quiet living room, but, paying it no mind, I snag my backpack for the roll of duct tape, flipping it in the air when I find it, catching it above my head, and, yanking at the sticky grey strip, I begin binding his wriggling body to the recliner.

Snaking the tape through and around the wooden arm with continuous crude ripping noises, I tug persistently on the strip, looping it around his left wrist and forearm, and, satisfied he won't be able to free himself, I don't bother cutting it once I'm done, instead, I start binding his chest, circling him and the chair thirty times before proceeding to his right arm. I do have to cut the tape to restrain his legs, though, so I rip it with my teeth and move on to those while the mustachioed gentleman brazenly explains the downsides of the pill. "You may experience loss of smell, shooting pain, trouble sleeping, numbness and tingli—" I zone the silver fox out again, fasten his right leg to the footrest and do the same to his left, going only as far down as his shins, because the unwashed yellow toes with the overgrown nails disgust me. Switching back to the baseball game, the TV returns to an acceptable volume, prompting me to visualize him thirty minutes earlier, watching the game, relaxed, with his feet up, buzzed and yelling at the umpires, drink in one hand, cigarette in the other, no idea what was in store for him, and, wanting to finish so I can get to the good part, I stand behind him, doing my best not to touch his greasy hair as I arrange his head so that it's facing

168

the ceiling. I loop the tape around his forehead and the headrest eight times before angling it a centimeter or two below his lips, maintaining its firm tension while I force his mouth open and wrap his chin, and, when I finish and back away to inspect my work, I'm amazed at how efficiently I was able to secure him to the Lay-Z-Boy, especially with him convulsing throughout. With barely any tape left, I look for an excuse to use it, somewhere I missed, but in my enthusiasm and vigor, my attentiveness to detail, I can't find one—he's completely bound to the chair—so I toss it on the floor, watching it roll towards the dining room table, where it stops and spins out when it meets a couple of cigarette butts on the dirty carpet.

Confident that he's thoroughly subdued and I'm not going to be caught, at least not in the next twenty minutes, which I estimate is all the time I'll need, I slide into the kitchen cool and carefree, no longer fearing what was plaguing me preceding this, the entire trip here—this is now inevitable. It's going to happen. There's a green and brown stew-like mixture in a pot on the stove near the bottles I'm planning on using, a whisk stuck in the crusty film that's formed on top, and out of curiosity I pull on the wobbly refrigerator handle, squatting to see what's inside: expired hamburger meat, fermented milk in a bloated carton, moldy cheese, a case of beer, bacon bits—and unimpressed, I let the door shut on its own while wrapping my arms around all five liquor bottles, hugging them against my chest on the way back to the recliner, unworried by the clinking glass.

With only one of the bottles unopened and the rest containing various amounts of whiskey, I line his elixirs up on the floor next to the chair, positioning them so that their labels are facing me. I don't recognize the majority of the names or characters on them—a crow, a goblin, a man wearing a top hat and carrying a cane—and, still in the ray of sun, the colloid of frozen dust surrounding us, I kneel to his level, gazing apathetically into his flickering eyes for a moment, spotting my reflection in his iris, then, with a smirk and a wink, I snatch the orange funnel from my backpack, shove it into his waiting mouth, and, unconcerned as to whether I damage a single one of his stained, rotten teeth, I jam it down his throat. He awakens, coughing, choking, and trembling, then registering that he's bound to the chair, he fights as best he can to move any part of his body, violently jerking his hands, arms, legs, and head, but it doesn't do him a bit of good as he carries on, unaware of what I know: that he isn't going anywhere.

Indifferent as to which whiskey I choose as long as it's not the unopened bottle—I'm saving that for last—I reach blindly for any of the others at my feet and feel the light weight of the near-empty one in my hand as a player hits a home run, sending the crowd into a frenzy, and, happily aware that there's still four more bottles to go, I flip the top off, tilting the bottle I'm now noticing is made of plastic over the funnel while staring into his eyes, which, fixated on me, are widening. Clenching his fists and flexing his arms and legs as I hold the funnel stable, it doesn't take long, maybe three seconds, to drain what's left, what I'm guessing, because I don't drink, is the equivalent of six or seven shots, eliciting several chokes from him, neither intense nor major (he's probably already had that much to drink today), but I'm patient and we're just getting started, and, not about to be disappointed, I fling the bottle behind me, hearing it bounce off the stairs and hit the front door as I fervently grab the one with the crow on it. Out of nowhere, I recall the girls from this morning, forming a mental image of the dark birds they were drawing on the sidewalk, and, given the tremendous luck I've had all day, the fact that I've arrived this far, along with the other things I've deemed to be signs that what I've chosen to do today is justified, I wonder if this is another indication of that, possibly some sort of omen, but as quickly as I concoct this theory, I decide it's merely a coincidence, **WORC DLO**, then, upending the bottle with an eagerness that causes me to miss the funnel at first, I spill an ounce or two on his face and on the cushioning, but I grin and keep pouring, my exhilaration growing as ounce after ounce flows into the funnel, swirling in a small pool at the bottom and disappearing as he coughs and gags, brown liquid sporadically shooting out of the corners of his mouth, dripping from his chin and onto his shirt, which is beginning to reveal sweat. Straining his neck and jaw, he grips the wooden armrest hard, digging into it with his fingernails and scratching out skinny grooves that reveal the raw, white wood underneath, and, realizing that brute strength isn't going to free him, he tries to sway like a child on a swing, thrusting his legs and torso in rapid, choppy motions with what little room he has to maneuver, accomplishing nothing more than shuffling the Lay-Z-Boy a few inches.

It's safe to judge by his choice of home décor—the deer heads mounted on the wall, the taxidermized animals frozen in silly stances on the hearth, the gun cabinet in the dining room, the predominately hunting-related magazines strewn across the couch—that he fancies himself a macho man, the type of person who's most definitely envisioned a

171

fictitious scenario involving a thief breaking into his home and bragged to his friends while downing a drink in a bar about what he'd do to the unlucky bastard who tried it, and this, especially, pleases me—I scoff at the idea, picturing him in a dingy, dimly lit bar before noon, grabbing fistfuls of peanuts out of a bowl with his unwashed fingers, demanding another shot as he fires up a cigarette and describes how he would take the law into his own hands, when my thoughts are interrupted by the abrupt rise in volume on the TV. A smug, smiling lawyer points in my direction with both index fingers, his colorful suit shining in the Sun, and he talks as if his audience were fifty feet away, detailing the types of cases he prosecutes in a deafening tone, explaining how you won't pay a penny if you lose, he only charges *when* you win, breaking my focus, so I scan the floor and table for the remote, and, not finding it, I march over to the TV and yank the cord out. I should have unplugged it earlier, but I don't let this minor inconvenience affect my high as I resume feeding him what he loves and enjoying the sight of his incessant, worthless struggle, unable to imagine how frustrating this must be for him, not the act itself, but the fact that he, such a manly man, can't do a thing about it, that he's going to be forced to endure it, much like an alcoholic's wife, unsure when—or if—it will end.

I sneak a final glimpse of the crow as I shake out the last bit of liquor, then sling the bottle at the raccoon, knocking him onto the carpet and shattering the glass against the brick. Now that there's no noisy TV distracting me, my jovial mood requires some entertainment, so I start humming, Elvis's "Such a Night" while dancing in place with my usual awkwardness—arms out but elbows glued to my sides, swinging my shoulders, my hips not really doing much—and I merrily scoop up the third bottle between weird, rigid moves, spin the cap off in a single smooth motion with my thumb and begin pouring. This half-full bottle has a label with a goblin perched on top of a barrel drinking, and, while repeatedly singing the only lines of lyrics I know as the chorus calls for it to myself, I begin humming more emphatically when he vomits. Already heaving wildly, his chest starts throbbing spastically as glops of puke splatter out of his mouth and snot bubbles up in his nostrils, the guttural noises emanating from his throat becoming harsher and more disgusting when, suddenly, a thick red liquid containing chunks of whitish meat begins spilling from his mouth every five seconds or so, mixing with the brown liquid and leaking like soup overflowing from a bowl as he thrashes in the recliner, going nowhere, his outbursts diminishing in vigor, making me wonder how much fight he has left in him.

When number three is empty, I whack the fox out of his sad, preserved stance, but the bottle remains intact, barely missing the hearth to land on the carpet and spin, then, in what I'm guessing will be his nonphysical attempt to persuade me to remove the funnel from his throat, stop what I'm doing, listen to what he has to say, he mumbles some weak, incoherent, whiny, pathetic garbage through the orange plastic. Looking terrified and vulnerable, tears trickle from his bloodshot eyes, blending with the sweat that coats his pleading face while he waits for an answer, hoping his solicitation will inspire sympathy in me, but unsurprisingly, it doesn't, as a matter of fact, his quiet petition only stirs up an extra, unexpected surge of emotion I wasn't aware

I had, motivating me to happily snag the fourth bottle without a care in the world and shake it mockingly in front of his bewildered eyes as they follow the whiskey sloshing back and forth inside the glass, prompting his expression to quickly return to one of anger and he reverts to thrashing around like a caged animal, but, unlike an animal, he has the ability to reason, to understand where this climactic epoch in his life is heading. I hold the bottle vertically as brown liquid gushes out of it in big chugs, complemented with a persistent glugging sound, while he persists with what meek thrusts he can, his bursting attempts to free himself getting weaker, further apart, and then what I'm assuming is bile based on its greenish color spews from his bluing lips along with the variety of white, yellow, and crimson chunks that are being discharged in heavier waves, the menagerie of colors and textures cascading down his chin and neck onto his already drenched shirt, soiling and saturating the sweat-soaked black fabric to the extent that a puddle has formed above his belly, submerging the fisherman.

Chucking this bottle at the fireplace, I don't see or hear it shatter because I'm too busy staring into his sedated, pitiful eyes as they close, his endeavors to free himself now abandoned, his convulsing body periodically spasming at seemingly patterned intervals, the faint jolts roughly ten seconds apart, suggesting that these aren't merely involuntary responses, he's at least partially conscious, and, delighted that he's still with me even if only marginally, I snatch the unopened bottle I saved for the finale, the label on which I absolutely do recognize. There's a stopper at the top that I don't yank out because I'm in no hurry and I want to savor this climax, plus the rising pool in his mouth is asking for additional time to drain, and, his dull, subdued eyes open partially, then close, then—scarcely—open once again, and they stay like that, trembling in their sockets, with the rest of his body quivering constantly as I tilt the bottle and keep on pouring to guarantee he'll get every last drop no matter what condition he's in, when I realize that I've abandoned my humming. Departing this world with several shivers, his subsiding murmurs are a series of gurgling noises that resemble the weak, liquid-filled breaths of someone who's drowning, and his body relaxes into the Lay-Z-Boy for good, which, is perfect timing, because, like him, the whiskey is finished, the last tiny bit dribbling after his last ounce of life leaves him. Instead of attempting to smash this bottle like the others, I simply drop it, barely registering its thump against the carpeted floor, then, drawing in a deep, long breath, I shut my eyes and crack my neck. The moment I exhale, it feels as if the weight of the world has been lifted off my shoulders, the ineffable sense of relief washing over me knowing no bounds and, when I open my eyes, it takes me a second to gather my thoughts, and absorb that what's just happened is real, before it dawns on me that I'm actually done, I've rectified everything, and shuffling to the couch in a dreamlike state, I plop down.

The cluster of magazines I don't bother to move crunch under me as I stretch my legs onto the glass coffee table, cross them, kick the mug at the edge onto the floor, spilling what I presume is alcohol-related, and recross them as bits of life from outside that I'm certain I didn't notice until now on account of the commotion in here creep through the thin walls—birds chirping, two, maybe three women talking, a vehicle's door slamming, an engine starting. Not paying mind to any of it, as if it were the regular, late-Thursday-afternoon neighborhood commotion I was accustomed to, I finger the magazines around me, scanning the covers. Hiding amongst towels and scattered copies of *Guns & Ammo*, *Hunting*, and *Deer & Deer Hunting* are pornographic magazines with "barely legal"-labeled teens on the front, their nipples concealed by cartoonish neon stars; several issues of *AARP* with celebrities posing and smiling, surrounded with bold-lettered topics of concern such as "Should I Quit My Job?", "Best Cities to Retire In", "Must Do One-Day Vacations", "7 Ways to Make You Feel Smart, Sexy, Pain Free", "Money Boosters", "Decode Your Belly Signals", "Dating After 50"; and last month's *Boating*. Detecting the stale, terrible smell of the house again, I look up at the weak ceiling fan, doubtful of its purpose, when, suddenly, he expels a sharp, abhorrent noise as his chest shudders and a heavy glop of polychrome liquid spurts from his mouth. Unfazed, I flip through the pages of the single issue of Boating magazine, hardly registering what's on them before stopping at a classified section advertising boats for sale, and disinterestedly skimming the images and ads with exorbitant prices, I rip out a page, scrunch it up tightly, and shoot. Not even close. I've overshot the funnel by six or seven feet and to the right, so I tear five more pages one by one, badly missing those attempts as well, then, figuring I'll get better with practice, I rip out twenty. While scrunching the pages into balls and setting them in a pile on the towel beside me, I think of a fantastic expedient, and, judging the distance, I bend my elbow at ninety degrees, aligning my shots before launching them into the air, and the ensuing three bounce off his stomach and knee, then a hip, the next hits nothing, disappearing behind the chair, only the eleventh and twelfth show signs of a chance, both ricocheting off his wet head after the preceding seven miss in a variety of ways due to my lack of prep, most too short, but the thirteenth shot, and I swear I know it the instant I release it, nails its target perfectly, landing in the funnel with a pleasing thwack—so perfectly, that I have no desire to attempt another. Confident that my delicate luck won't get any better, and exceedingly ecstatic about my spontaneous idea, I slap my knees and stand, then head to the kitchen to begin my hunt.

I'm more than positive that there has to be an anonymous one here that I missed earlier—forgotten or hidden in a cupboard, by dishes and cups, under the sink, or up in the back of one of the hard-to-reach shelves, maybe the freezer—and I scour all of these places twice, even rummage the fridge in vain I scanned twenty minutes ago, but I can't find anything. Disappointed, I'm now thinking that being unable to perform this closing act will sour the taste in my mouth, lessen the magnitude of what I've done, so I consider cutting him loose, sliding the shades open, and flinging him through the window, when it suddenly dawns on me. I head down the hallway, the wood beneath the worn-out carpeting creaking with each step, and push on the warped door to his musty bedroom, where his bed is unmade, two of its pillows resting on the floor against a giant black tool cabinet that's lined up alongside the wall on my right, the sunshine sneaking through the blanketed window reflecting off various silver lug nuts and wrenches organized in rows in the drawers, and, past that, on top of the nightstand, next to the alarm clock that's blinking a menacing red "12:00," is exactly what I need. Disgusted by the cover of the porno magazine under the almost full bottle—the slightest idea of him doing that in here repulses me—I glance aside while grasping the glass handle and catch a glimpse of a hamper full of dirty clothes and a pair of boots caked in mud lying on a pile of camouflage hunting shirts and pants, all previously hidden by the immense toolbox, and twirling around to return with an excited gait, *creak*, *creak*, *creak*, into the odorous living room, I reach over him for the green lighter he no longer has any use for.

I grab a small bath towel from the assortment on the couch, twist it, and shove it in the neck of the uncapped bottle until half of the cloth is soaked in whiskey—the perfect incendiary device—and set the remaining mini-basketballs on fire, ensuring they're well-lit so they won't go out on their own before I toss them enthusiastically everywhere—into the kitchen, at the TV, in the vicinity of the table and gun cabinet—then, flicking the tip of the lighter, I let the tiny flame burn as I take in one last satisfying view of the man bound to the Lay-Z-Boy, and, igniting the towel, I heave the bottle at the fireplace, shattering the glass. Huge, wild flames spread swiftly in all directions, consuming the drapes and walls, flanking the brick in a matter of seconds, and navigating the carpet, a rogue line of fire reaches his recliner, instantly igniting the old, booze-drenched fabric, engulfing him in bright yellow and amber flames, the crackling blaze scorching and burning his hair, clothes, and skin right in front of my eyes. With the rampant inferno expanding much quicker than I'd expected, the room becomes remarkably hot as a great deal of smoke builds around me, and, realizing that I need to get out of here while I can still breathe, I snatch my backpack with the utmost urgency and sprint to the door before I won't be able to find it.

Brilliant blue skies, the Sun, and, more importantly, fresh, clean air welcome me when I rush out onto the front porch and stumble down the stairs coughing, indifferent about the cracks on the sidewalk and my disheveled state because of my pride and eagerness to record my final deed of the day on paper, to show that I've completed what I was determined to do today, so, eagerly pulling my diary out of my backpack, I scribble this last entry, covering it with two broad, swooping red strokes. Oblivious to what's transpired at her neighbor's residence across the street, the elderly woman who greeted me when I arrived is on her lawn chatting it up and laughing with a lady her age who spaces her hands apart to demonstrate the size of something, then rubs her belly. She beams when she notices me by my bike, her eyes widening as she nods with approval, her expression morphing to a quizzical look as if to ask if my surprise was successful, and being that it was, I humbly but mischievously grin in response, when a startling, thunderous explosion booms from inside the house, echoing in the air. Simultaneously flinching and embracing one another the two women are overtaken with shock, and their gazes drift slowly in sync from the burning house to me, their mouths agape, and, once again, as if they're a two-part act, one unable to perform without the other, they begin backing away from me in unison, their stuttering feet leaving and hitting the ground rhythmically, unable to believe what they're witnessing. Unsympathetic to their reaction, I sneak an extra peek behind me at the ranch home as smoke billows out the front door and chimney and seeps through the windows, the immense, unruly flames spreading to the roof, then, turning back to face the stunned seniors with that same smirk, I shrug and pedal off, my cruiser squeaking like it has all day, and, with horrified expressions contorting their faces, the two women scurry down the driveway, their elbows interlocked.

cherish – verb : protect and care for (someone) lovingly **ethereal** – adjective : extremely delicate and light in a way that seems too perfect for this world **serendipitous** – adjective : occurring or discovered by chance in a happy or beneficial way **weltschmerz** – noun : mental depression or apathy caused by comparison of the actual state of the world with an ideal state **euphoria** – noun : a feeling or state of intense excitement and happiness

anthrodynia – noun : a state of exhaustion with how shitty people can be to each other **aurora** – noun : a natural electrical phenomenon characterized by the appearance of streamers of reddish or greenish light in the sky, usually near the northern or southern magnetic pole **endure** – verb : suffer (something painful or difficult) patiently **heartmoor** – noun : the desire to feel things intensely as you once did once did **rückkehrunruhe** – noun : the feeling **yu yi** – noun : the primal longing for a home village to return to a of returning from an immersive place that no longer exists trip only to notice it fading rapidly from your awareness

THIS MORNING I'D HAVE BEEN more than content with just being able to finish what I started today, but now that I've gotten this far it's not enough; I must get home so I can appreciate my last moments in a place I recognize and want to be. It's 3.18 miles to my house, the Sun seems to be shining the brightest it has the entire day, and at the pace I'm planning on averaging I figure it should take twenty minutes as I swing a left onto Carey Street without signaling, not paying much attention to where I am, my fantastic state and yearning for home causing me to round the corner too wide, briefly veering into the path of a green station wagon that's roughly twenty yards from me. Not making him brake and nowhere close to him, I correct myself, waving to accept blame, admit "my fault," but with no consideration for human error or for my apology he beeps at me before throwing his hands up and giving me a mystified look. In maybe half a mile, while passing a community pool, I find myself wondering how long those ladies, who I'm confident by now are on the phone with the police, have known each other. Are they great friends or merely acquaintances? Do they share meals or converse solely when they catch each other outside? Do they celebrate each other's birthdays with thoughtful gifts purchased months in advance, or do they have to be notified by Facebook? Do they take trips together or have they never driven in the same car? Are their conversations meaningful, joyful, and sad at times, or feigned, fleeting statements regarding the weather routinely added to the occasional hello?

I've only had two friends in my life, what I consider real friends—individuals who were truly kind to me and genuinely cared about me, who would always sit patiently every time I introduced them to a song or movie scene I found amazing while polling their faces and waiting for them to enjoy the cool parts. The rest of my associations—superficial, ultimately shallow, no risk of joy, sacrifice or loss—were simple acquaintances I certainly could never call or count on when needed. I wish there were a "previously on" button for life, akin to the beginning of a TV show that restarts after months off the air, that, when pushed, reminded people how nice or pleasant or fun someone is and can be, that they're worthy of more than what's being given at the moment, so it wouldn't be necessary for them to see that person again to remember, possibly forging a stronger conversation or a higher probability of meeting up purposefully in the future, perhaps friendship. The problem with today is that good, decent humans aren't cherished, they're used, and much like the melting ice caps and warming oceans we're facing, we know what's going on and also how to alleviate it, but we choose not to, the majority of our decisions based on greed, desire, hate; two fight for one and then there are none.

These impulsive notions have put me in a weird, hazy state, but I snap out of when the light ahead changes from green to yellow, impelling me to quicken my pace, and, once I've beaten it and crossed the intersection, I can't for the life of me recall why I'm in such a rush, why I'm feeling so awfully anxious about getting home. Unsure why I'm experiencing a momentary lapse of reason, I retrace my thoughts of the last several minutes and beyond until I finally remember why I'm pedaling so furiously: I have no idea how long it will be until the police find me, no clue what information they've learned. Will they be around the next corner?—prompting me to shake my head in a way that convinces me I'm clearing my brain and resetting it to guarantee this won't happen again. Now, definitively aware of the root of my concern, my restlessness grows as I approach a line of vehicles stuck behind a garbage truck that's turning left across oncoming traffic, so I search for anything positive to occupy my mind with while cars honk and a black Audi SUV attempts to drive through the inadequate, marginal space between the truck and the edge of the sidewalk, as I manage to single something out: the swish fulfillment of sinking that thirteenth shot. Veering closer to the smelly truck to avoid any further erratic behavior from the agitated driver in the SUV, I squeeze by, picturing that crumpled piece of paper floating through the air in slow motion, hearing the sound it made when it landed, and, following that, just what I need: My thoughts are flooded with serendipitous factors and elements that aided in today's success—the unlocked doors, Mason not arriving five minutes earlier, uninterested neighbors, quality headphones, the distraction of porn, the condition drinking left two people in, a shovel in an opportune spot, soft earth, nobody stopping and discovering me at the comic shop, the bodega empty except for the two people I wanted to be there, the day's weather defying the forecast—convincing me that there's no reason to worry, it wouldn't be a fitting ending, me face down on the asphalt, my wrists forcibly and tightly cuffed while passerby record it with their cell phones. I will make it home.

Braking roughly two miles from my house, there's another line of vehicles, of seven—no eight—cars and SUVs belonging to twenty- and thirty-something parents, all parked halfway onto the curb, waiting for their children to scamper in a chaotic cluster out the main entrance of the daycare, their arms extended, backpacks as big as them bouncing up and down behind them, when all of a sudden, a dented Toyota truck whizzes by me, beeping at the last car in line, the driver flipping off the row of vehicles while speeding past and swerving across the solid yellow lines in the middle of the road before he takes the next right, three streets ahead of the one I'm turning onto. Baffled by his idiocy, a disapproving, elderly husband and wife in sweaters and polyester pants and aerobic shoes, sitting on a black metal bench, revert their eyes to the little students and parents and educators, but instead of waving again, they simply smile, happy spectators watching kids be kids, parents be parents, young women in the prime of their lives and at the beginning of their teaching careers, and when they're both satisfied, which seems to be at the same time, they stand, eventually clutching one another's hands as they amble towards the moderate, grassy hill that leads to Bull Branch Retirement Village, inducing me to briefly imagine them repeating this ritual every weekday—notifying each other of the hour as they drink tea in the kitchen of their spotless condo, eagerly anticipating their weekday walk, then passing the rows of newly built brick buildings and fenced-in pool with interlocked fingers while exchanging silly and fun stories of their children and grandchildren when they were that age, before settling early at their usual vantage point to ensure they don't miss out.

The twenty minutes I had to travel shrink to ten, I'm on Kenwood, then Hickok, steering onto Vermont, coasting to the bottom of a hill, ten minutes dwindles to five, through an intersection without stopping or signaling after checking both ways, to Jefferson, turning onto Poplar, then, before I know it, I'm zooming around the corner I've sped by a thousand times, slinging my leg over my bike, balancing on the right pedal like I did as a kid, going down and up the ditch, under the tree with the swing, jumping off, letting my cruiser land somewhere on the lawn, and surprisingly, maybe unsurprisingly, there are no police here; my house and my neighborhood are as I left them this morning—except for the better weather—still quiet and peaceful, nobody outside. Breathing moderately hard, I stare at the split-foyer that I've lived in for two decades, picturing it the way it used to be—brown, wood siding, blue gutters, and window shades that matched the doors—and, like every day, it feels as if this morning, my exercises and rituals, my breakfast, my leaving this yard, took place recently, an hour ago, but it didn't. It was all a part of a Thursday that's whizzed by with no delay, now a memory, triggering another memory, of the time my mom told me one Sunday at Melvin's over breakfast when I was in high school about what my grandfather warned her of at the hospital the day I was born: that this stage of our lives would be gone in the blink of an eye. And this reminds me of the senior couple on the bench waving at the three generations they once were—children who can't fathom they'll grow up, parents who believe they never will, and young teachers who are oblivious to the fact that someday they'll be sixty—no doubt both amazed with the whirlwind it all came to slip by in, how days became months and blended effortlessly into years. My house gradually morphs back to its original form—white, vinyl siding, green shades, gutters, and front door—and, elated that I've made it home, I dash across the driveway, scaring a flock of cardinals out of the bushes near my mom's white, rusted station wagon. They fly east then change direction, soaring over a wooded area until I can't see them, and, as I sprint to the top of the stairs on the back porch, the exact opposite of my zombielike state this morning, I trip on one. Prior to stepping inside I take in a last, fond view of the lawn that I mowed on Monday while chuckling at my predictable, comical mishap, then the pair of green, plastic chairs and empty table in the middle of the deck meant for drinks, snacks, and card and board games, and, not necessarily truly desiring it, probably just so that I can use the word, I tell myself that the ideal, perfect ending, would be if it were a little later in the evening, and the Sun was dipping beyond the line of mountains in the distance the way it always does, and its red and pink and purple lights were fading to a dusky fuchsia.

When I slide open the glass door, the familiar, pleasant scent of home smacks me in the face, and, after giving it a few seconds I inhale again, deeply, slowly, trying to get an additional hit, but it's faded, weakened, making me wish I could identify and cherish it as intensely as I did initially, that I'd experience that sensation no matter how long I was here, but, like a mother whose child's laughter once brought great joy, jolted her awake from her daily routine, it's been diluted, and has already reverted to being a passing, everyday occurrence. It doesn't matter much anymore, I guess, but the stench from the fire is lingering heavily on my clothes, I need to remove them, so I kick off my shoes, wriggle free of my backpack, and unzip my jacket, hanging it on the coat rack. Now unconcerned with my hair, I run my fingers through it several times, gently massaging my scalp, concentrating on the crown of my head, a quirk I have that unwinds and relaxes me, when, for the briefest of moments, out of habit, I listen for a greeting, some sense that I'm finally here, but predictable silence is what I get, and my silly, purposeless yearning evaporates as fast as it came—I'd accepted days ago that I could no longer return home.

Regardless of what I've done during the day, I ordinarily jump in the shower the instant I arrive home, foregoing everything else, whether I'm fixing or eating dinner, playing video games, watching TV—the fresh feeling of washing off the day provides an extra, comforting contentment to whatever I'm doing, plus my hands are dirty, sticky and dotted with soot, and I'm just realizing that I've put this in my hair. Knowing I won't be able to fully relax and process the day in the living room without one, and maintaining a slightly fortuitous attitude on account of today's circumstances working out perfectly and my not being caught yet, I untuck my shirt and start pulling it over my head to save what little time I can while hurrying across my kitchen, which has been the same for years, past the table with the black and red checkered table cloth and the green, pea-shaped salt and pepper shakers resting on a pod in the middle, the red blender used for milkshakes, smoothies, and soups, the decades-old microwave that's never developed an issue, the various porcelain angels aligned in a row on a wooden shelf above the stove, the reddish kettle meant solely for tea, the pumpkin-shaped cutting board, all things that were always easily identifiable but had become undiscernible in the last week, as if they were foreign objects I had no right to touch, to the refrigerator.

I keep the Cokes in a row at the bottom of the door, and so it'll frost up in however many minutes my impromptu shower takes, I snatch a Tupperware bowl, fill it with water, drop in the can and a handful of ice cubes, set it in the freezer, grab my jacket, and, unbuckling my belt and unzipping my pants, I scramble down the stairs. Hurriedly undressing and bouncing on one leg, I almost fall when I yank my left sock by the toe while looking for the stain on the ceiling, which, oddly, I can't find, and when I step in the shower it still seems small, but not as tight, as if what I've accomplished today has earned me some meager benefit. Between shampooing my hair and washing my face I hear Magnum barking faintly and I picture him halfway through his door, then me in bed, next, my exercise routine, breakfast, and, like the trailer for a movie, the rest of the day plays out in no particular order as the green and purple tiles gradually vanish—me leaving the yard, my bike squeaking, a sullen shot of the dreary clouds panning to a video-game perspective from above, Chris and Mike talking and joking as I enter and hoist a shotgun, Chris smashing into the wall, Mike's head exploding, Remi teasing me while I hug the package, the bloodied, muscular man and scrawny guy in the tub both screaming madly, the viewers unable to discern what's being done to them, and, to add sex appeal, trashiness, comedic value, and beauty, a bit of intrigue, the blonde high school senior in a pink bikini bouncing and swaying her tanned legs, the Asian woman on her stoop, lingerie showing, the elderly lady on her balcony, the retired fisherman, the entitled driver in the white Mercedes honking her horn and yelling with a silly, contorted expression, the serene, picturesque garden with the beautiful colors, scantily clad prostitutes, beggars waving signs, a park full of people, me flying across the galaxy, the cat purring and rubbing on my legs, Mason peeling around the corner in a flash, his squinting, curious eyes following me, a house burning... all concluding with me cycling home under a radiant sky shining while approaching the lawn on one pedal, into the kitchen, then here.

Unable to recall the last few minutes once I come to, I'm not sure if I washed my face, so I do it immediately before drying off as best I can, swiping recklessly at my body and flinging the towel haphazardly on the rack, and, barely parting my curls, I apply a hasty dab of pomade, slicking it back with my fingers in lieu of the brush while taking swift, rushed strides to my dresser and throwing on the synchilla pants I habitually wear when I'm relaxing at home, a V-neck t-shirt, and a fresh pair of thick socks. Glimpsing specks of red I hadn't noticed until now dotting the shirt I ditched on the carpet with everything else, I inspect it, but against the pink fabric I can only make out what resembles a spilt condiment or sauce, and, indifferent about those or the flecks splattering my jacket and pants, without considering the hamper, I kick it all into a pile. I check again, but the stain isn't on the ceiling, so, choosing not to sweat it, wonder why, or whether it was ever even there to begin with, and hankering to get to the living room, I jump the stairs two, then three, at a time.

With a thin sheet of ice surrounding the Coke when I open the freezer, I walk it cautiously to the sink so I won't spill any water—something that, currently, should be the least of my concerns—empty the plastic container, lay it on the rack, grab the family-size bag of peanut M&M's from the freezer, my backpack, then once I'm in the living room, which is dimly lit by what remains of the day outside, and now conclusively and absolutely relieved, I collapse onto the couch. I place the can on a coaster from Melvin's, stretch my legs onto the wooden and glass coffee table, cross them, recross them, and, unaware of what colors I get, I toss two, four, occasionally six M&M's into my mouth together between sips of Coke—it doesn't really matter how many as long as it's an even number—when I suddenly remember that I haven't looked at my phone in over an hour and a half. Disregarding several calls and texts from various local numbers I don't recognize, I open Harry's messages.

"Oh my god, Schroeder," the first one reads. "What have you done?" And, "Please call me so we–"

But I don't read the rest or worry myself with anything else my phone is telling me, instead I flick it onto the couch, watching it bounce off the cushion and onto the floor, and pop two more M&M's into my mouth while absent-mindedly observing the room I dusted and vacuumed yesterday even though it didn't require it. It was already exceedingly clean—pristine, actually—I just needed it to be perfect for this evening if I made it back, plus it felt like the type of place that deserved that, the kind of room that must be nothing short of unblemished given the way I now viewed it. I take a swig of Coke, burp quietly, and thumb the pages of the Homes & Gardens magazines laid on top of one another on the sofa table to my right like a hand of cards so you can catch a glimpse of each cover, then shift my gaze towards the recessed bookcase in the wall and the various photos of different moments of my life and my mom's.

Positioned in groups of three and forming triangles at both ends on each of the five shelves, there are framed images of us at a petting zoo, playing putt-putt at a church gathering I can't recall, my high school graduation, us dancing at a wedding last summer, my lapyear, the age I became older than my mom was when she gave birth to me, all of them in chronological order starting at the bottom shelf, with items from my childhood scattered between the frames in mom's style of organized chaos—a worn, brown harmonica, baby socks, my first report card, yellow and blue science ribbons laid on sports team participation certificates awarded out of sympathy to neutralize any sadness or disappointment related to not receiving a trophy, a tiny Swiss army knife, an arrangement of eight miniature stuffed animals circling a clay figure I'd molded in third grade that was supposed to be a dinosaur, my first pair of glasses. On the second shelf there's a circular, framed picture of us at the lake, I was maybe eight, with puffy, dark hair and a big smile, mom's wearing a red skirt, a matching tank top, kneeling and hugging and swallowing me whole; in the orange frame beside it, we're eating sandwiches on the tailgate of her station wagon, I remember that it had rained, and, after scanning each of the pictures on the shelves again, for the first time in my life, I realize these aren't only snapshots of me growing up, but my mom as well.

I don't want to, but ignoring my emotions and instincts I allow my eyes to shift impulsively to the left, past the ugly golden mirror I'd bought my mom years ago with my birthday money at a yard sale, a gift she'd proudly hung on the wall that afternoon, to the maroon recliner, then the four-foot-tall antique wooden radio next to it. Drifting into a groggy, sorrowful mindset, I chuck M&M's into my mouth mechanically and raise the can of Coke to my lips out of habit, no longer appreciating the taste of either, so in an effort to redirect my progressively worsening mental state, I glance around the room while doing my best to concentrate on anything other than what is preparing to flood my brain. I visualize the people I killed today in a nondescript setting yesterday, excitedly anticipating their possible weekend plans or a trip scheduled months in advance, all of them oblivious of what was to come, but that fades instantly when my useless, distracting thoughts return, my eyes glazing over as I find myself gawking helplessly at the vacant recliner across from me while waves of anguish and dread roll in, gently, at first before, inundating me and crushing the sense of relief and bit of joy I ridiculously believed I had earlier. Striving to hold on to a thread of what I'm beginning to accept was truly a minimal, transient bout of delight and solace brought on solely by the attainment of redemption, I feel like I've just returned home from an immersive trip only to notice it fading from my awareness, as if it was all a dream, and, already knowing that it won't work or grant me the lasting satisfaction I desire, I try to put it in context and start picking apart my fleeting happiness, but the illusion continues to dissolve until it's totally lost, my temporary euphoria extinguished, and because it's going to occur no matter how I attempt to stop it, my eyes slowly move from the beige carpet to what's sitting on top of the radio.

Favorite songs that were often listened to in this room begin playing in my imagination, as if they were coming from the radio's speakers, all of them at a low volume, one roughly superseding the previous one with loud static in between—first Elvis, then a line from a classic country ballad we loved, "Jingle Bell Rock," "The Girl from Ipanema," "Beyond the Sea," "Adagio in D Minor," and, finally, "Time to Say Goodbye", **EYBDOOG YAS OT EMIT**. Convinced I've reached that juncture, I rise sluggishly, missing the coaster when I set the can down, and, shuffling reluctantly towards the radio, my steps heavy and sedated, I carefully lift the magenta and ivory marble urn I'd chosen last Wednesday from the selection on the wall in a room filled with coffins for sale while bawling uncontrollably in the presence of a man and a secretary I'd met five minutes prior. Smooth, slick, and polished, the colors mixing and flowing together, it had stood out among the available options, giving me the impression of being the most elegant, fitting representation of her. After staring blankly at it for several moments, what she said concerning the urn during our last dinner in her hospital room pops into my mind. She'd deliberately skipped any type of solid meal and requested that I bring her six scoops of fudge ripple ice cream in a bowl instead. She ate the whole thing.

"I want you to pick what you like, sweetie. That's what has always mattered to me."

Backpedaling lethargically to the couch, I bump into the edge of the coffee table and collapse onto the cushions while struggling not to cry, the roof and back of my mouth soon getting sore from straining to accomplish this, and, taking quick, irregular breaths, I try to construct a favorable memory of us, and I can, a myriad of them in fact, but each one is short-lived, too transient for me, lasting only a second or two before it's ousted and replaced by the next, flashing by unable to pause, so in a desperate, last-ditch bid to prolong what minute, positive, comforting sensations linger, I look to the collection of happy photos snapped during predominantly traumatic times that I can be sure won't disappear, but now, along with the rest of the room and the house, like it has been since my mom's death and since the moment I walked in here, they and the radio, the empty recliner, the horrid golden mirror, the candy dish I'd drain fast regardless of how often she filled it—objects that should be familiar—seem unfamiliar, as unrecognizable and distorted as the recording of mom's voice I'd transferred to Alexa in a weak attempt to still hear her. Knowing she'd want it, I force a smile, hugging the urn against my chest, rubbing it softly, and she feels incredibly light, inadequately weightless compared to the body she occupied, which is why it's so bafflingly difficult to fathom that it's actually her in my hands, and the only way I can make sense of what happened is to say that she was too perfect for this world. Her death affected me tremendously, the pain surpassing anything I could have ever conceived, the idea of her not being here becoming so unpleasant, so unbearable, I knew I didn't have the strength to overcome it. The next blank, thoughtless seconds turn into minutes, how many I'm not sure, until a distant noise catches my attention, snapping me out of my fog. Barely able to register the sounds of the sirens and surmising they're on Jefferson, maybe the beginning of Poplar, I straighten up and regain my composure, astonished that when I wipe my cheeks, there's nothing's there. Setting her on the coffee table, I position the urn so her full name and the dates delineating her time on Earth, all stenciled in uppercase amber lettering, are facing me, and grab today's notebook from the backpack at my feet.

After planning my route yesterday, I organized all my diaries chronologically, stacking them in two neat piles on the Windsor chair in the corner. On Tuesday, it took me the entire morning to discern and highlight in yellow dozens of entries from them, entries I'd deemed as accurate, descriptive accounts of various atrocities my mom and I had had to endure since I was a child and she was a young woman—records that, once exposed, I hoped would offer a glimpse of what our lives entailed, help whoever reads them to understand why I did what I did.

But maybe not. Laying this latest diary on the most recent pile of yellow notebooks, I align it evenly with the others, the sirens growing louder—they're definitely on Cornelia by now—then, removing the gun I'd brought along today in case of emergencies from my bag, I bounce it up and down in my palm, recalling how much heavier it felt when I first held it years ago, my teenage mind oblivious to the devastation and mayhem it was capable of causing, incredulous of the power of such a small device to end a life.

I want to have four M&M's and one last sip of Coke, so I do, in that order, and I can't help but wonder about the same question I'd once feared and continually asked myself over the past three days: What will it be like after death? Like before I was born? Nothing? Darkness? Possibly a scorching, boiling Hell where I'm perpetually ripped to pieces for eternity, wailing in agony forever as a result of my actions today? Or a heaven that for predictable reasons I've always visualized with lots of clouds and dazzling, brilliant beams, a utopia my mom and I can exist in free of pain? I long for the latter more than anything and used to fear the first two with a horrible dread, but while falling asleep in bed last night, my comforter yanked over my head, I was able to convince myself that it ultimately didn't matter—why fear something that can only exist when I cannot? And with this final thought, as if it came right on time, not a moment too late or too early, both Magnum and Sam start bellowing at the previously faint sirens that had steadily risen in volume and were now deafening in my front yard.

I don't bother to check or switch my position at all, unconcerned with the red and blue lights that are flashing outside my window, their reflections flickering off the glass over the framed photos, but I do briefly picture the neighbors scrambling onto their lawns in their robes and sweatpants, or whatever they wear once they're settled in for the evening, curiously checking to see what's going on, their cellphones recording. Several orders are barked out and quickly met with affirmative responses preceding the stomping of feet on the front stairs. Following that, I hear fast, heavy steps storming up the back deck, reverberating through the wall, and I'm ready for the familiar sound of the sliding glass door in the kitchen, but it doesn't come. Instead, the next thing I hear is an officer yelling my name twice from the other side of the front door amidst mad banging on the wood, then whoever I'm assuming did the knocking and shouting requests permission to breach the perimeter while I crack my neck with the same ease with which I did in the house I burnt to the ground. I adjust my glasses, take a deep breath, exhale calmly, slowly raise the gun to my open mouth, inserting it gently, and I know that life is truly a gift I should cherish, one where if we only knew food and sun and water and shelter, that's all we'd need, it's beautiful if you think about it, and I'm well aware that when the public learns of this, even after the content of my diaries has been revealed on the news, online, and in the papers, a great number of people will still emphatically express their opinions, saying, "He should've just skipped to the end," that my apathetic, unforgiving obligation to involve the victims was unwarranted, and an insignificant, weak man like me not only destroyed the lives of the deceased, but the families as well, and I'd considered that multiple times, and there could have been a reality in which that was the case, except that didn't seem fair. Despite the persistent, broken scenes in what has passed for my life and my constant, nagging state of exhaustion with how shitty people can be to one another, I've always tried to see the beauty and good in the world, sought to think the best, but with what devastated me last week I just don't understand this place anymore, and I sincerely believe I have no connection deep enough to pull me out of the abyss I'm in. My life has become something I could never have imagined, something I never intended: a nightmare I was suddenly thrown into fraught with a terrible, abysmal sadness comprising of mixed, pessimistic sensations and disparate emotions and feelings I don't want to feel anymore, and I'm relieved I won't have to wake up tomorrow morning disappointed to find the world the way it is.

March 18, 2008
deer Diury,
this is my first entre! I am ten and I luv my mom
and comics and pizza but not dad he is mean to us
and hurts us.

March 24, 2008
deer Diury,
nothing to report good exsept the same stuff of
lots of yelling and hitting and crys.

April 10, 2008
dear Diury
I sleep with Sweet Lou last night for the first
time! After we ate brekfast together I put him
to the window so he would get too look at things
while I was at school. David locked me in my
locker again today. He also took my puddin at
lunch. When I got home mom was crying like alwaze.
We sat on the porch and ate pizza. Dad came home
falling. He yelled for hours and hit mom. he
yelled more and hit me. This happens a lot. I wish
he wasn't here.

June 29, 2008
dear Diury,
today is my birthday! I am ten! mom and me are
gone to the lake!

dad ruined my party at home and smooshed my cake

with moms face and popped all the baloons he tryed
to throw sweet lou away but mom got him.

July 22, 2008
dear Diury,
dad hurts me and mom a lot.

Septermbr 9, 2008
dear Diary,
David put catsoup in my seat at lunch. I sat down
and it got all on my pants he called me a girl and
said I was on my periods. the kids laughed. at
dinner dad pulled sum of moms hair out and kicked
her cause she dropped his drink.

Octobr 14, 2008
dear Diury
Today at school we painted. I drew a picture of
a flemengo. Dad ripped it to peeces when I got
home becuz it was pink. More yelling and screams
tonight when im in bed. Dad smells funny and
only shouts or sleeps a lot. Mom cried a lot. She
sleeps with me a lot.

Octobr 22, 2008
dear Diary,
Today was sonny and nice but not for long. Mom and
I tried to

sorry Diary. dad just left. he hit me over and

204

over. im sad and in pain and don't want to write.

Novembr 21, 2008
dear diary,
David keeps telling me that I'm a mistake and that
all the others think I smell and nobody likes me.
I cried a lot but mom says im not that and she is
so happy to have me. Dad kicked mom today in the
stumach becuz his dinner was cold.

Decembr 21, 2008
dear Diary
Dad beat me bad becuz I woke him up. I didn't mean
two but I broke a glass. The kynd doctur says I
need to wear the cast for six weaks and now dad
calls me a pusy but I don't know what that is.

Decembr 25, 2008
Chrismas was very bad. Mom went to the hospital
becuz of dad.

January 5, 2009
dear diary,
Today at school David peed on the slide and made
me go down it. My pants were wet and I cryed. At
home dad called me a girl when I cryed about it
and hit me hard.

January 13, 2009
Dear Diary,

David pushed me on a red ant hill at school and shoved me in it. They got in my cast and I had to go to the hozpidal Also Mom and I played a game today. We went to a hotel and ate McDonuld's. The room was way up and high. She shakes and cries a lot. The phone rings but she tells me not to answer we're still on play mode. Sweet lou and mom and me watched Diznay cartuns til late.

January 24, 2009
Dear Diary,
I did a funny joke on mom and froze pickle juice and gave it to her like a popcicel. she made a face and it was sooo funny. I tried with dad but he hit me and kicked me so hard. he is never fun or nice or kind.

February 5, 2009
Dear Diary,
Today my cast was cut off. Im glad becuz it itchd a lot. Mom took me for ice cream after. When we came home dad was loud and shouted at us. He hit mom twice and called me that pussy word again. I know what it means now becuz David told me. Mom says I am not. We went to my room an he left us alone.

October 13, 2009
Dear Diary,
I know it has been a while and I'm sorry. I am now

in the seventh grade and not much has happened. Dad went to jail which was perfect. It was for the last two weeks and it was like a vacation for mom and me until he came back. Now it is just more of the same. He hit mom this morning and she can't see straight and feels dizzy. He has only been back for two days. I guess one day of luck is all we can hope for. It's sad. At school David makes things terrible. I don't want to go. Highlights of just this week:

He tripped me in the cafeteria and I fell and spilt my tray and food everywhere

He threw me in a garbage dumpster

I got a swirlie on Tuesday

And basically every, single day I get hit in the head when I least expect it - this seems to be his favorite. He just sneaks up behind me and punches me in the back of the head. Five times so far this week.

Anytime I start to cry he enjoys it so I try not to, but it's hard sometimes.

November 30, 2009

Dear Diary,

I have a concussion. David hit me so hard today outside of school that I blacked out. My head is hurting so bad. Dad threw alcohol on me at dinner when he got back from work at the garage, and asked me if I was gonna cry like David asks.

Then he warned me to stop complaining and smacked

mom when she tried to take up for me.

December 25, 2009
Today is Christmas! I am up at 5!

Mom and I opened presents and I got a glove and comics and a watch with Mickey Mouse on it. I gave mom two drawings I made. Dad didn't speak the whole day. He just sat in the corner watching tv. He knocked over the tree and smashed plates and ruined all of it once it was night. Him and mom shouted all day and into the night. I cried and I didn't want to because I was supposed to be happy.

February 18, 2010
David hit me in the face with a rock today at school. He and the kids call me mean names like loser and gay and tell me I'm ugly and annoying and no one likes me. The nurse was sweet and her clothes were bright and clean. When I got home dad hit me a lot with his belt for no reason like usual. Mom tried to stop him but he hit her too. We always sleep together now.

March 11, 2010
David stole my new Mickey Mouse watch and dad hit me with his boot today in the head when he found out I lost it and I woke up on the kitchen floor. He also slapped mom because his dinner was cold. Then mom and me drove around the neighborhood in

the car until I fell asleep.

April 12, 2010
Today was bad at school. David yanked my pants down and forced me to dance for the other students. It was at recess and no teacher saw it. I wish he'd stop. I hate school because of him.

May 11, 2010
David punched me in the stomach today and spit in my face. He punches me every day and steals what he feels like in my lunch. Yesterday he threw it all in the garbage. Mom and I watched a funny movie before bed. Dad has been gone for two days and we have no idea where he is. It is so nice when he is not here. I hope it stays this way.

July 17, 2010
Mom is in the hospital. Dad hit her a lot and she has a cast on her arm and bruises on her face. I do not want to be here alone with him. He is happy and then suddenly mad so I stay in my room. Mom is supposed to come home tomorrow. Me and Sweet Lou are going to play video games til late.

September 6, 2010
David came up with the name Schantelle for me in the first day of school today and now that is what all of the students call me, even two of the teachers. I don't understand why this happens.

I'm a kind person and good to people. I don't deserve this and I have to go to school and face this every day. I keep telling myself that the next year will be better but so far eighth grade is just as bad as all of the others.

November 25, 2010

Today is Thanksgiving. Mom and I went to Cracker Barrel and had a yummy meal together. After that we drove around to avoid going home. Of course, dad was drunk when we returned. We were hoping he'd be passed out or asleep, but we weren't that lucky. He banged mom's head against the wall and smacked me a few times. He seems to love telling me that I'm a worthless piece of shit while doing this. Mom told him she was going to leave him and he yelled that he would kill her if she tried.

Jan 9, 2011

Last night was awful. Dad came home from the bar late when mom and I were already asleep. He fell down the stairs through the door and beat mom with the broom when he woke us up and she came out of my room. I found her curled up in a ball in the hallway and when he asked me if I felt like doing something about it, I got on the floor and hugged her until he went away. He did, but not before telling me that I was a loser and would end up just like mom.

June 6, 2011

This is the last week of middle school. So far it has been terrible. Earlier in the week David poured milk on my head at lunch in front of the entire cafeteria. On Wednesday he dumped his tray on me and today in gym he had his friends hold me down in the locker room while he peed on me. When I informed the gym teacher, he called me Schantelle, too, and told me that if I was going to cry I should go outside. I feel like I can't get any type of support or help anywhere except from my mom. I'm miserable at school and with my life right now. The only good thing I have is my mom.

September 5, 2011

Today is my first day of high school! I am hoping that it will be a lot different than middle school! I will update.

David broke my nose today. He and some of his friends jumped me in the woods behind school after classes. They threw my new backpack in the creek and broke my glasses. I don't know why he treats me like this and does these things. I've never done anything to him. It has always been this way and it doesn't seem like high school will change that. Mom and I went to Melvin's for dinner after the hospital and we have an appointment to see the principal, Mr. Osborne, tomorrow. When we got home, dad was drunk in his Lay-Z-Boy watching baseball. He kicked mom in the stomach because she didn't bring him something to eat and then he punched me hard in the chest, knocking the wind out of me. I felt like I couldn't breathe for a while and it took minutes for me to catch my breath.

Mom and I are now at some cheap hotel on Wards Road. It's not nice, but much better than being at home.

September 7, 2011
Mom and I went to see Mr. Osborne today about David. He told us that he can't punish him if I don't have some sort of proof. He said he talked to the other boys and that none of them saw what I accused David of. He added that David's dad owned half the town and I need to suck it up and something about kids being kids. Mom cried in front of Mr. Osborne and mentioned dad and what he's been doing to us. They're good buddies and drink together so he laughed and blamed her, and he had the nerve to say that she must have done something wrong. His advice was for her to be a better wife and that she should suck it up too and that all marriages aren't perfect. He thinks dad is the man of the house and we're in the wrong by not listening to him. Mom cried some more but he just laughed at her. I have no idea what to do

now. On the ride home mom was extremely upset and said she can't tell anyone else now after the way Mr. Osborne reacted, plus she's worried he might tell dad.

June 13, 2013
Today is my first day with my first job at the country club. I really hope it goes well.

The day was terrible. Everyone was very mean. All of the members were arrogant and unkind to me and so were the employees I worked with. David is a member at the club so I know that will not be good. While I was at the concession stand he poured a bottle of soda on me from behind and then put me in a headlock. The members and guests and other employees that were around just laughed. I felt so ashamed. On the way home, he hit my bike with his BMW and pushed me off the road. One of the rims is ruined now. Dad has gotten even worse if that's possible. He put Mom in the hospital again and she had just returned home. He is already yelling at her after drinking all day. Every time I try to help he either punches or slaps me too. I wish there was more I could do, that I was able to stand up for us and face him. We are going to the courthouse tomorrow. Mom is filing for divorce and getting a restraining order.

July 19, 2013

Today was not a great day. I had to be at the country club at 5am for an annual tournament. When I got there I found out I was David's caddie and he shoved me in the lake on hole #2 in front of dozens of members and guests. No one helped me or thought it was mean. Everyone just laughed. My clothes were soaked for the rest of the tournament and it was miserable. He started calling me Schantelle and by the end of the day even some of the adult members were calling me that.

September 28, 2013

Dad is gone. The police were here today and made sure that he left. He was polite at first, but that's only because they were here. He called my mom a fucking bitch and yelled out to me one last time that I would never amount to anything before he slammed his truck's door. Once he left, mom and I cut the grass and hedges and we planted some flowers as well. Mom showed me a lot of plants and I think horticulture is something that truly interests me. A class is taught at school and I'm going to take it next year. We also cleaned the house from top to bottom. It and the yard are so much cleaner. We had the windows open all day and it smells a lot better inside as well. After we finished for the day we cooked pasta and ate on the back porch. We reminisced over old memories like trips to the lake and when I was in elementary school. It was nice to remember that stuff but it also brought back bad memories that surrounded them, which I didn't like.

October 14, 2013
David has been telling all of the other students at school that my dad left my mom because she is a slut and was cheating on him. Now everyone believes him and other students say things to me and give me nasty notes with gross drawings of her. I am having panic attacks at school now when I see him. I start to tremble and can't breathe. Will this ever stop?

December 4, 2013
David and his friends forced me off my bike again with one of his BMWs today. This time I hit the asphalt and scraped up my face badly. It looks like pizza so I'm staying home from school for a couple of days. Mom said it's ok and that we will hang out together. She bought a gun today in case of dad because he has been calling and telling her he is going to kill her for leaving him. She took out the bullets and when she handed it to me it was so heavy. It's hard to believe something like this can take a life so fast.

December 11, 2013
David had someone from the special-ed class draw a picture of me today with my face resembling

pizza. In lunch he stood on a table and got all of the students' attention, showing it around. He yelled that everyone should call me pizza face and that's what they did for the rest of the day. I was so ashamed and embarrassed. I went to the parking lot and cried for the rest of lunch. On the way home, him and his buddies sped by in his BMW SUV throwing bottles and rocks at me. One of the bottles hit my temple and now I have a terrible headache.

Jan 7, 2014

Mom and I went to meet with Mr. Osborne today concerning David and the twenty dollars he stole from my locker. Mr. Osborne said there is no proof and that there was no reason for me to have brought that amount of money to school in the first place. Plus, he says David's dad is rich so he doesn't need to steal. When mom brought up the rest of the things he had done Mr. Osborne said we had no proof, then he told me I need to just suck it up. He also had the nerve to mention that if I had a better mom I would not be like this. While looking right at her he claimed she was weak and that dad was a good man and he was right to leave her. He even said they were out last night together!

October 14, 2014

I saw mom crying for the first time in a while

today. I was fixing us dinner when she came home very upset and all she told me was that her new manager touched her a lot today while making comments detailing a lot of gross things after requesting she work late and massage his wrinkly, tattooed neck. I asked her what else he said and did, but she wouldn't tell me. She just took a long shower and then we ate a quiet dinner.

November 11, 2014

David set up an email with my name and emailed the most popular girl in school, Sarah. In it he said nasty things and sent crude images, too. She confronted me at lunch today about it in front of the entire cafeteria, screaming and showing the pictures. I was so shocked I didn't know how to react. I just sat there as everyone else laughed while she yelled at me. She had no idea it wasn't even me. I tried to tell her and Mr. Osborne but I was suspended for a week. He told me if mom was a better mom I would not be this way and I need a real man like dad around and that I am probably like this because I read kids' comics. I felt so much shame and it's so bad because I didn't do anything. The only thing I enjoy there is horticulture class. I can just be by myself and tend to the plants.

April 7, 2015

Mom lost her job today. She had worked at the

same company for fifteen years. She was crying in her station wagon when I returned home tonight from band practice. Her dress was ripped and she told me that after all the employees had left for the day the sleazy manager touched her again and shoved her to the ground when she refused his advances, and then forced himself on top of her. She didn't specifically say what he did, but she said when he was done he told her not to come back and that she was fired. She cried the entire night while I hugged her until she fell asleep.

May 22, 2015

Mom has been trying to get a job but she can't. The man who attacked her won't give a reference so we are getting food stamps so that we can eat. Dad came back last night banging on the front door. He was drunk. We sat in mom's room and she held the gun til he left when the police came, which wasn't long, but it seemed like it was. Afterwards we watched some TV, but mom was extremely nervous and repeatedly checking outside the window to see if he was coming back. He didn't.

June 2, 2015

Today after basketball in gym David and his friends stripped me down until I was naked in the locker room and tied me up in athletic tape. Then he sprayed deodorant in my face and stuck a pencil in my butt. They videotaped it with their phones and sent it to the rest of the school. I am so mortified and ashamed and can't believe this is still happening to me my senior year in high school. Mom and I went to meet with Mr. Osborne today about it. He alleged there was no proof of where it originated and that you can't really see, much less make out any of the "so-called" perpetrators in the video, and he ended with, "suck it up" telling me there's only one month of school left. It makes my skin crawl when he says those three words. Mom was visibly upset, but he just laughed like he always does. He doesn't care at all. He even had the nerve to touch her leg and ask her to dinner and drinks.

April 5, 2016

We have been on food stamps for a year now. Mom still hasn't been able to find employment anywhere and it worries her a lot. She is stressed out constantly and it's taking a toll on her. She's tired a lot because of this or dad's phone calls or late-night visits where he bangs on the door. Also, David is home from college for spring break. Last night he and his friends bashed our mailbox in and toilet-papered the tree in the front yard. This made mom even more nervous because she was thinking of me. I cleaned all of it up and went to buy us a new mailbox. After that she and I sat on the back deck and played cards. We ordered a pizza and it turned out to be a nice day in the end.

Oct 1, 2018

I started a new job at the fancy bodega, T. Hardy's, that recently opened. So far it has been good. There is a huge Black guy there named Harry who works in the deli. He's awfully kind to me and today we had lunch together on one of the picnic tables in back.

July 13, 2019

A new comic shop opened in town. I can't believe it! The owner, Remi is so cool! Tonight, we organized some of his comics and ordered burgers and fries from the restaurant across the street. He's got this tan, leather chair that looks as if it belongs in the 70s in his office and he bragged about how it was in some film I haven't heard of. He also showed me some new comics he had received yesterday. I had never seen The Amazing Spider-Man #1 in real life before! It was very cool! I'm really glad that Remi moved to town and I met him. His family is from India and he's the first one to live in the US. He went to college, but dropped out to open the store which didn't please his parents. But he told me he was adamant about wanting to be happy every day doing something that he enjoyed because life was short, and he doesn't regret his decision. He seems quite happy to me. It ended up being 3:18 AM when I returned home. I tucked mom in and slept in the chair next to her like I do every night in case she needs anything.

June 15, 2020

Tonight was my fifth year high school graduation reunion. I wore a suit and tie that I'd bought with money I'd saved up, but David and his buddies poured watered-down feces on me in the parking lot before I got in and ruined any hope I had of attending. They tackled me out of nowhere and he stood there laughing with a bucket. I was able to sneak inside and take a shower without my mom seeing me. When I went back to her bedroom she was in bad shape and propped up on her pillows. I lied to her and said that I had a fantastic time and it was fun to reconnect with some old friends. I'm sure she knows I was lying since I never had any friends. She doesn't look healthy. She's weak all the time and her hair is falling out. We have another appointment with the doctor tomorrow.

February 22, 2021

Things have not been going well. Mom is sicker and my job at T. Hardy's has not been great. The new guys that started last month, Chris and Mike, are awful to me at work. For some reason they find it funny to see how many times in a day they can surprise me with a punch to the stomach or a jab in the side from a broomstick. They keep count. They don't do it when Harry is there though because he sticks up for me and stops it. Tonight Harry took me to dinner at the EL Rodeo and told me all about his wife and two kids. He once worked in the document shredding industry but it kept him away from home, and he got this job so he could be close to his family and see them more often.

October 1, 2021

Mom has been throwing up a lot and getting sick in the middle of the night. Last night we were in the bathroom for two hours. We were recently accepted into a program, so a charity is paying for a nurse to be here during the day while I'm at work and two evenings. I had an extra four hours tonight so I went to the comic shop. Remi and I ordered a pizza and watched The Thing, his favorite movie. It was quite good. He was impressed with the condition of my The Amazing Spider-Man #3. He said he would give it a 9.5, which pleased me. For some reason he has started calling me "fool" as a nickname, but the way he says it is funny, so I don't mind at all. He told a bunch of comic-con stories tonight and showed me some photos of him and some women. I like Remi a lot. He actually listens when I talk and we share several common interests. He has travelled to a lot of countries. He's going to Europe next summer and he even asked if I wanted to go! I couldn't believe it! But I'm also sad. I'm not sure it's something I can afford. I really hope his comic book shop does well.

January 27, 2022
Chris and Mike cut the tires on my bike today
to show off for the new girl, Maggie, who's a
senior at the high school. The three of them were
waiting and laughing at me and smoking when I
came outside. When I questioned them about it,
Chris smacked me in the face and got extremely
close to me, acting as if he was truly going to
hurt me and I believed him because of the way
his face changed. Walking home David was driving
the opposite direction and he veered towards me
honking his horn and flipping me off.

January 28, 2022
I notified the manager, Todd, of what was done
to my bike yesterday. He said there was nothing
he could do without proof. Harry heard about
it and he had a talk with Chris and Mike and
Maggie, but after he left for the day, the three
of them warned me that I'd regret it. To make the
day worse, mom and I ran into dad today at the
grocery store. Like always, he had been drinking.
He followed us out to the parking lot, shoved
me against the station wagon, and grabbed mom's
arm and called her a cunt for divorcing him. She
tripped on her walker and fell to the ground.
She has a purple and blue bruise on her forehead
and at the hospital they informed us that she
had a sprained wrist from where he grabbed her.
Tomorrow we are going to the police station.

March 19, 2022

Chris held a knife to my throat at work today and threatened that he would kill me if I went crying to Harry and out of nowhere Mike struck me in my kidney, causing the knife to cut my neck. After bandaging it up I lied to Harry when he asked me what happened and told him that I cut myself shaving. I am still shaking over all of this while I write. Maggie had not gotten there yet but I heard them telling her the story and she thought it was funny. She replied with, "He deserves it. He's a fucking loser." Every single time she has to deal with me, she talks down to me as if I'm an idiot and unworthy of her time, posing in this "akimbo" stance that she continually uses when addressing only me and no one else. I still have no idea why they hate me so much and do this. I've always been nice and made an effort to talk to them.

June 22, 2022

Tonight I went over and hung out with Remi again. It's the third night this week I've been to his shop. He's painting the inside of it and rearranging some of his sections so I offered to help. It's been a great way to get my mind off things, plus I enjoy helping him out. When we were done painting we ordered a pizza from Rocco's and then had a Rubik's Cube competition. I destroyed him. His best time wasn't even within a minute of my worst. I had a lot of fun, but I kept thinking about mom and I felt a little guilty for not being home, but she told me I need my own time as well, and it's nice but I still feel bad.

July 18, 2022
Maggie kicked me in the balls today for no other reason than to get Mike and Chris to laugh. Which they did. They called me a pussy and added that I should quit, that no one wants me around. Later in the day she slipped something into my drink that caused me to vomit violently for almost an hour. I have no idea what it was, but I'm still sick. I also had a present I had bought for mom early in the morning before work, a porcelain angel for her collection I was going to surprise her with that I had wrapped with a ribbon, but Chris smashed it on the floor and then I had to clean it up. I don't know what else to say about how I'm feeling right now. Just not good.

September 1, 2022
Mom is not doing well and our nurse is on suspension, so I can't go to work but Harry told me not to worry, that he will cover my shifts if the manager has a problem with it. He also surprised me with an angel because he knew I couldn't afford a new one! I didn't know what to say. What a great thing to do for someone. Mom loved it. Remi came by to visit her tonight. He

brought an old movie she liked when she was a kid and the three of us watched it together.

December 12, 2022
I went back to work for the first time today after having to take two weeks off to look after mom because our nurse was fired for showing up to jobs drunk and they had to find another one for us. Chris and Mike harassed me my entire shift, asking me when my mom was going to die and if they could come to our house and fuck her before she did. Mike kept saying she could take both of them, and Chris said he loved older women, that they had experience and she probably enjoyed anal. Maggie acted as if she was genuinely sad for me, coming close to me to console me, then she kneed me in the balls. Mike shouted, "score," and Chris suggested they should start the game again. I started crying and tried to run out of the store, but Mike tripped me and I fell into the wall which made them laugh even more.

January 13, 2023
Mike pushed me into the street today when a car was driving down the road in front of work. I was sweeping the parking lot and he walked out next to me as if he had something to say concerning the walk-in cooler and then he shoved me. Luckily the car was slowing down for the stop sign or it could have been a lot worse. The elderly lady driving

didn't see what happened and that I was shoved and of course Mike is denying it. Chris and Maggie weren't there but they lied to Todd and said they were and that I tripped and fell into the street on my own and that it was my fault. My knee is banged up really badly. It's hard to walk and I need to pay for the woman's windshield, which is $329. My savings only has $537, so that is not good. I can't imagine I'll ever save enough for the trip to Europe with Remi.

February 27, 2023
Chris and Mike and Maggie told me I should kill myself today. That I was not a man and everyone would be better off if I did it, including my mom. Chris asked if that was the reason she was sick, because she had a pussy for a son and she was ashamed of me. I didn't know how to respond. I couldn't even cry. I felt like I wasn't even there.

April 9, 2023
Today I was at the grocery store and saw David. Just seeing him caused me to start to breathe hard and sweat. He saw me and screamed out Schantelle and then all of the customers and employees around us turned to stare. He ran up to me and poked my side, hard, telling me I had a skinny-fat body while reminding me that I was a loser and probably no one still liked me. Then he wrapped

his arm around me tight and bragged about his newly bought mansion and two BMWs while still poking me and he wouldn't let me go and I just stood there trembling and started feeling dizzy. I wish I was stronger and was capable of standing up for myself, but I can't. I was already having a bad day and this made it worse. This morning Chris pinned me against the sharp pebble wall in the back hallway at work, scratching my face, so of course David pointed that out. He brought up the pizza face drawing in school, then made a nasty comment about it being a disease from my homo comic boy lover. Some customers and employees were staring and laughing but no one intervened.

May 25, 2023
Todd called me this afternoon telling me not to come into work tomorrow. He notified me that Maggie had filed a complaint that I touched her inappropriately and tried to force myself on her after I pulled out my penis. This never happened! I would never, never do such a thing! She also lied and told him I have been saying crude things and ogling her since her first day of employment. He said it had to be taken seriously and certain steps had to be followed because she was going to the police. He added that Chris and Mike had backed up her story and that they said they had witnessed it and she had complained to them before saying she didn't know what to do while

crying. I just can't believe what is going on. Why would someone do that to another person? I didn't tell mom. She is in such bad shape that she doesn't need to hear this. Harry called me and told me he'd help me if he could. He also sent some flowers to mom and had dinner delivered to our house.

May 26, 2023

Maggie called me today screaming into the phone when I answered. She shouted that she was going to the police station next week to accuse me of trying to rape her, then she hung up. After that Mike and Chris left some mean text messages calling me disgusting and a pervert. Todd called around noon and told me he was sorry but I'd have to be let go. He also informed me that due to the nature of my firing he wouldn't be able to give me any type of reference. I don't know what I'm going to do about a job or money now and I'm terribly worried about what might happen with the police.

June 17, 2023

I have no idea what to do. At the police station they informed me that Maggie was pressing charges after her family hired a lawyer and I'd need to return, most likely to be arrested. The lady wasn't sure when and now I just have to wait. I'm so worried. I have no idea what to do about it. On top of that, mom is in the hospital.

It's just terrible. I have spent the past four nights here. Remi and Harry visited today. Remi brought another movie and Harry brought dinner so we wouldn't have to eat the hospital food. Mom enjoyed seeing them. She didn't feel good, so she couldn't eat and she fell asleep halfway through the movie, but both Remi and Harry still stayed til the end.

June 19, 2023
Today mom looked better. She was surprisingly hungry, which was a positive sign. She asked for ice cream, so I bought her favorite - fudge ripple. She ate the entire bowl and fell asleep with a smile on her face while I held her hand. Tomorrow she's supposed to undergo more tests and the doctors said they will have more answers after that.

June 20, 2023
Mom died this morning. It was awful. I was asleep when the machines that monitor her started beeping loudly, and some nurses ran in quickly with a doctor. I stood in the corner shaking and just watched, but she didn't have anything left in her. She just laid there with her eyes closed and head tilted to the side. There was nothing they could do. Yesterday she was here and now she's gone. I feel so lost. I don't think I have anything left either. I can't stop crying and

shaking and I don't know what I'm going to do.

June 23, 2023
Each day is worse than the last. Two days ago, I picked out mom's urn and now she's on the radio in the living room. I can't believe this is my life now. It's like I'm in some terrible nightmare and I have no idea how I got here. The feelings I'm having are awful and sad and persistent and I just want them to go away. I'm having constant headaches and taking Ibuprofen three and four at a time to try and ward them off, but they're not helping much. All I do is stumble around the house half alive/half dead looking at things I don't recognize. The most important person in my life is gone. The only person to ever truly cherish and love me. I feel so lonely so lonely so lonely.

June 24, 2023
This afternoon an epiphany dawned on me while I was sitting on the porch in a fog. What Sam did for Magnum I should have done for my mom and myself a long time ago. I know what I'm going to do. Now I just need to plan it.

June 28, 2023
I think I'm ready. I've packed everything I need for tomorrow and just finished mapping out my route. I'm hoping it won't rain like it did today but it doesn't look great. I had lunch with Harry

and Remi yesterday, which was nice. Harry was very consoling and so was Remi, but in his usual, humorous way, trying to get me to smile with some of his silly antics. Harry still believes the emails I'm sending him from the fake Gmail account are real so tomorrow morning he'll be two hours away at a radio station to collect a fictitious $10,000 prize he thinks he's won instead of at work after I send him the email in the morning. Remi's package is also ready. I organized all of my comics in chronological order and placed them in a big, cardboard box. I could never have imagined giving them away in a million years, but Remi should have them. I'll put my best one, The Amazing Spider-Man #3, with the rest after I read it for the last time over breakfast. I'm going to miss them both. I'm well aware that Remi and Harry are real friends and good to me, but I also know they won't be able to pull me out of this. No one can. As far as who I'm visiting tomorrow goes, I don't have any feelings about that. When I read the parts I highlighted in these diaries it made me so sad and those people made the choices that brought them where they are. I figure this is my final entry, so I'll end by saying I just can't make any sense of how my life turned out or of this world and the way it is, and I don't understand how human beings can be so mean and awful to one another and cause such pain with such disregard. I can't continue riding some wave wherever it takes me, and it's heartbreaking to me that this is where we are, alone in a dark corner of the universe, and this is how we treat our own kind.

Chapter headings words and definitions:

(S) – fester (v.), riddle (n.), nadir (n.), labyrinth (n.), petrichor (n.); (C) – lagniappe (n.); (H) – diaphanous (adj.), phosphene (n.), aquiver (adj.), bellow (v.), toned (adj.), kerfuffle (n.); (R) – gossamer (n.), idyllic (adj.), bombinate (v.), iridescent (adj.); (O) – syzygy (n.), picturesque (adj.); (E) – porn (n.), flow (v.), sequoia (n.), euphonious (adj.), silhouette (n.), nefarious (adj.); (D) – saunter (v.), quintessence (n.), dulcet (adj.), akimbo (adv.), effervescent (adj.); (E) – defenestration (n.), ineffable (adj.), epoch (n.), wafting (v.), incendiary (adj.), elixir (n.); (R) – endure (v.), ethereal (adj.), serendipitous (adj.), aurora (n.), cherish (v.), euphoria (n.)

Retrieved June 29, 2024, from https://www.oed.com.
(Oxford English Dictionary, 2024:online)

(S) – altschmerz (n.), 2/9/2019, zenosyne (n.), 12/28/2022, paro (n.), 3/7/2019, des vu (n.), 6/6/2021, koinophobia (n.), 12/13/2021; (C) – trumspringa (n.), 7/10/2022, xeno (n.), 3/24/2013, heartworm (n.), 2/27/2020, kenopsia (n.), 6/28/2020, rubatosis (n.), 3/21/2016; (H) – whipgraft delusion (n.), 12/13/2021; (O) – sonder (n.), 6/21/2019, ambedo (n.), 3/26/2021, monachopsis (n.), 6/21/2015, onism (n.), 9/7/2021; (E) – oleka (n.), 1/9/2021, routwash (n.), 5/6/2022; (D) – kudoclasm (n.), 6/19/2022, liberosis (n.), 3/7/2019; (R) – anthrodynia (n.), 2/17/2022, weltschmerz (n.), 7/14/2005, rückkehrunruhe (n.), 6/18/2020

Retrieved July 9, 2024, from https://www.urbandictionary.com.
(Urban Dictionary, 1999-2024:online)

(S) – aulasy (n.); (R) – wytai (n.), keta (n.), aimomonia (n.); (O) – harmonoia (n.), mahpiohanzia (n.), midding (n.), mimeomia (n.), volander (n.); (E) – vaucasy (n.), nemotia (n.); (E) – heartspur (n.), swish fulfillment (n.); (R) – heartmoor (n.)

from John Koenig's *The Dictionary of Obscure Sorrows* (2021).
Simon & Schuster.

(S) – epiphany (n.); (C) – taradiddle (n.); (D) – murmurous (adj.)

Retrieved July 9, 2024, from https://www.merriam-webster.com.
(Merriam-Webster, 2024:online)

(C) – evanescence (n.); (H) – sanguinolent (adj.)

Retrieved July 9, 2024, from https://www.dictionary.com.
(Dictionary.com, 2024:online)

(D) – youth (n.)

Retrieved July 9, 2024, from https://www.collinsdictionary.com.
(Collins Dictionary, 2024:online)

(C) – clinomania (n.)

Retrieved June 29, 2024, from https://www.wiktionary.org.
(Wiktionary, 5/27/2023:online)

(R) – Dracula monkey orchids (n.)

Retrieved June 29, 2024, from https://www.wikipedia.org.
(Wikipedia, 7/8/2024:online) & https://www.attozflowers.com.
(A to Z Flowers, 2017-2024:online)

(R) – yu yi (n.)

Mandarin translation

(E) – pilot pen g2-07 (n.)

Retrieved June 22, 2024, from https://www.pilotpen.us. (Pilot Pen, 2024:online)

About the Author

NEAL CASSIDY is the author of *the final weekend:
a stoned tale* and *SCHROEDER*. He was born in 1975
and raised in Forest. He is a graduate of The Nene
School and lives nowhere in particular.
Neal can be reached at nnaight@yahoo.com.

Also by Neal Cassidy

the final weekend: a stoned tale

In the last days before the real world, six college friends prepare to take a bow in epic fashion. After Sunday there's just Harry, the future business owner; Justin, the medical intern; Trent, the hapless wanderer; and Clarence, soon to don the badge and blues. But now they have years of memories to honor, all packed into one weekend. Will they grow into their new adult roles? Will they go out in style with the girls? Will the four of them even survive the sheer level of debauchery? Living in an apartment paid for by the Grandma, an ex-hooker turned millionaire, Courtney and Ling-Ling couldn't be more opposite, yet are completely inseparable. Courtney and Harry have been hooking, neither able to commit, but their imminent separation is about to test that arrangement, and Ling-Ling's never-ending reciprocated crush on Justin just might be more than that. Their lives intersect with that of Professor Goodkat, their idolized instructor who never quite "left" college himself. In Goodkat, we find the consequence of getting to live out a hedonist fantasy, and the possibility for change in anyone. Hilarious, raunchy and uninhibited, "the final weekend: a stoned tale" captures contemporary society while chronicling the dreams, regrets, perspectives, and future after youth in an unbroken sequence of shockingly touching exploits. No longer armed with the excuse of college stupidity, these friends will go on a journey with higher stakes than a night out has ever had. Because there are things about themselves that blacking out can't erase.